Purity

C.J. Lewis

AuthorHouse™ UK Ltd.
500 Avebury Boulevard
Central Milton Keynes, MK9 2BE
www.authorhouse.co.uk
Phone: 08001974150

© *2009 C.J. Lewis. All rights reserved.*

No part of this book may be reproduced, stored in a retrieval system, or transmitted by any means without the written permission of the author.

First published by AuthorHouse 11/20/2009

ISBN: 978-1-4490-1763-7 (sc)

This book is printed on acid-free paper.

What has been will be again, what has been done will be done again; there is nothing new under the sun.

Is there anything of which one can say "Look! This is something new? It was here already, long ago; it was here before our time.

Ecclesiastes 1:9-10

For all those who have suffered needlessly especially for Kim.

Part 1: Home.

"Man is the measure of all things. Of things that are, that they are and of things that are not that they are not."

(Protagoras)

Will you tell me a story? Asks the girl.

What kind of story, my angel? Says the man.

Anything. I don't mind.

How do you feel?

I feel well today. Tomorrow I may be worse.

Are you not tired?

No. I am not tired. But, tomorrow I may not be well. That is why I want you to tell me a story today.

For the sake of this story: How old are you?

You know how old I am. I am fifteen. With a bit of luck, I may be sixteen next year.

How old am I?

You know how old you are. You are very old. You are forty years old.

Ah, but this is our first problem! How old are we for the story? And, by the way, you cheeky little monkey! Forty is not that old!

What do you mean, "how old are we for the story?"

Age is such a funny thing, you see, says he. My heart always tells me that I am younger than my mind tells me I ought to be.

I see what you mean. Well, in that case, tell me a story from the heart.

That is fine, my angel. But, now we come to our second problem. You see, there are only so many tales to be told. For instance, do you want a story about boy meets girl, or do you want good to meet evil, or maybe a story about travel and excitement? Do you want a new story, or do you want a tale that is as old as the hills? A legend maybe? Or, maybe a fantasy?

Why a legend?

Because, my darling, in the greater scheme of things, human experiences are rather frail and limited and it is my belief that even legends are born out of the substance of human experience.

I see what you mean. In that case, I think I would like an old story with excitement, thrills, love and good and evil all in one. Let's say, a fantasy-legend story. That should be great fun!

Shall I tell you about the Spanish princess and the commoner?

No. I want to hear a new-old story. You have told me that one before.

How about a story about a young princess who has to combat against great evil?

Are all the odds stacked against her?

Most certainly, my sweet.

Yes. That will be fine.

You'll have to help me. I haven't thought this one through yet, so I am not sure where it is going. At least, since it is a fantasy, we can make our characters do what ever we want them to do.

Where is it set?

It doesn't matter.

Is it on this world or another world?

It doesn't matter.

When did this story happen?

Oh, a very long time ago.

Where does it start?

In the temple.

Who is the first character?

The oracle.

Ah! Good! I like the sound of that. Does he strike a very holy and frightening pose?

No. I don't think so. I think I would like my oracle to display some humour, or maybe even a tinge of cynicism.

How does he greet those who seek audience with him?

The first time he meets a stranger, he says: "I am what was; I am the here and now; I am the future; I am the truth; I am the mirror of my people; I am the Oracle; I greet you."

That is a bit ostentatious, or do I mean elaborate?

I think you mean, "elaborate", but I like "ostentatious". I always feel that "ostentatious" is a word that should be used about concrete things, like furniture or buildings rather than abstract or verbal concepts. But, there is an awful lot of furniture in his greeting, don't you think?

Yes. Carry on. What is his function? What does he do?

To him falls the task of chronicling the history of the royals when they die. This has now happened and our oracle will attempt to tell it as it was. He will write it all down in a scroll that will be placed at the feet of the deceased in the burial chamber.

His second task is to tell the future to those who wish to hear it. It is his opinion that great care should be taken in this matter, both by those who wish to hear what is to befall them and also by those who convey these supposed truths. It is exceedingly difficult, both to hear and accept the truth and also to tell it. Like criticism, most folk will accept the truth provided that it casts them in a good and favourable light. Being in his position, he frequently has to distort the truth according to the character of the person who wishes to hear his fortune. Even an oracle has to take care of his own skin!

She stirs: "What is truth?"

You may well ask. Truth as a concept is indeed very fluid. Do you not think that, as children we take a very simplistic view of truth? During the day we notice that the sun is shining, that the rain is falling, that flowers are growing and that birds are flying. At night we see the stars and the moon and we are happy. We accept these small truths and we do not ask for the whys and the wherefores. But, when we reach adulthood, we start to question the reasons for these events. Let's face it, even the most eminent scientists cannot always agree as to the truth behind these natural phenomena.

Was that you or the oracle speaking?

I was speaking for both of us. I will let him continue now.

Even in other areas, such as politics, truth is not easy to establish. If the king has to act on a difficult matter, he may call on a number of his advisors to instruct him. Each of these advisors will express the truth as he sees it in his own wise words. It will ultimately fall to the king to extract the little gold nuggets from each bit of advice and act on his own perceived truth.

Well, he must not complain. He is the oracle. He is supposed to be wise. To him falls the lot of pampering to the vagaries of human nature.

The body of the deceased is embalmed and will lie in state for a week. He has seven days in which to tell the story of a life. He has lit the candle and assembled his quills and scrolls. Where shall he start?

She brushes a strand of hair from her forehead: where do these people live? Describe their city.

That is a good idea, my love. Let's start with the city.

The city stands proud and magnificent on the high hill, surrounded by its walls. There are two entrances: one from the south and one from the north. Travellers always approach from the south where they are confronted by the two silver tigers, the emblem and guardians of the city. They are cast in the highest quality silver from the silver mines. They are perched high above the arch of the southern portals. It is said that, if you come in peace the silver tigers will fill you with awe and wonder, but if your intentions towards the city and its people are unfriendly, their eyes will stare down at you, filled with a malevolent gleam and they will cause apprehension to course through your veins.

The southern entrance itself is guarded by two gates. On arriving, the visitor is allowed through the first gate which is then shut behind him. After being questioned as to his purpose for visiting the city and (if necessary), searched by the guards, he is allowed to enter through the second gate.

The inner walls of the portals are equally magnificent. They are decorated with friezes of riders on horseback, dressed in the green and red cloaks of the cavalry. The horses all strike different poses: their nostrils flaring, some are seen to gallop, some to canter and step high, some rearing up on their hind legs and pawing the air.

On top of the wall, on each side of the portals, stand two high watchtowers. These towers are well lit at night and they are always well manned by the city guards. From here they have a grand view of the southern slopes of the hill and the valley below, as far as the distant dark forest. Any visitors would find it impossible to approach the city without being seen and inspected from a very long distance.

At regular intervals on top of the wall on either side of the watchtowers, are a number of defensive turrets that are at all times manned by soldiers. The front of the wall has an overhang of approximately six feet and on top of this overhang are embedded sharp metal spikes. All these measures are essential for the defence of the city, because it is affluent and prone to invasion from other cities and marauding bandits.

To the west, east and north of the city the landscape rises steeply by means of a series of sheer cliffs that form the base of the Mountain of the Spirits. So, as you can see, the city is near impregnable. To the south we have the watchtowers and its sentries, and for the rest, the mountain provides ample protection. The shear cliffs that surround the city would make it practically impossible for an army to circumvent the city without the most extreme difficulties.

There is another gate on the north side of the city. This gate provides an exit and entry to those who work in the silver mines and foundries. Because of the secure position of the city, this northern gate is only lightly manned.

The cliffs and hills surrounding the city are so rich in silver ore that, on a clear night, when the moon is full, the landscape glows with a dull lustre. Nearly all the inhabitants of the city receive their living from the silver works. There are some wealthy landowners who own the land on which the mines are located. The even more wealthy industrialists lease the mines from the landowners. There are those who provide slaves and other labour for the mines, the furnaces and the silver works. There are the silversmiths, craftsmen and artists who shape and sculpt the raw silver into the most wonderful artefacts in this land.

And, finally, there are the traders who sell the silverware in the shops and the market place. It has to be said, there are very many who would travel for months in order to purchase these most wondrous articles.

She sighs: It all sounds rather splendid and idyllic. Are there no poor people in the city?

Very few; only the elderly and the infirm. The king imposes a tax on the wealthy and the monies raised from this are used to maintain the city walls, the palace, the temples and all the other buildings of the state. It is also used to provide for the poor and the sick.

Oh dear. An ideal of a welfare state, I see. Who is in charge of all this?

The king.

Ah! The king! Tell me about the king. He sounds rather special. Be sure that you don't make this king of ours too good, otherwise I may not believe in him.

It is a myth-legend-story, my darling. You do not have to believe in your characters.

Yes, I know. But, is it not human to contain some measure of badness as well as good? If we should remove all the bad from our character, do we not in some way sacrifice our humanity? But, let me see what you make of the king first and then we may have another discussion on this matter.

Yes, my love.

The king is a fair, honourable and kind man. However, he rules with a firm but just hand. He takes advice from his council on all-important matters. Half the council is replaced every two years by election. Any adult male or female is allowed to stand for council and everybody over twenty-one is permitted to vote in elections. On matters of extreme importance, such as a national crisis, all adult members of the city are entitled to express their views. On these occasions meetings are held in the market place with the king himself presiding.

She laughs lightly. It sounds like a wonderful system and the king sounds too good to be true. Is it not unusual for a ruler to be so in tune with his people? Normally power corrupts.

Ah, but our king is different. Not all before him have been as enlightened. For example, during his grandfather's reign the silver industry had been badly handled. The mining and smelting techniques had been outdated and basic. Crafting of the silver consisted mainly in the form of a cottage industry. All this resulted in a low turnover and a lot of wastage. In spite of its dormant natural resources, the folk were poor and the city was badly neglected. The palace, the temples and the housing were poorly maintained and the parks and gardens were shoddy and unkempt. Although the king's grandfather was a benevolent man who was dearly loved by his subjects, he was also rather idle and lacking in ambition.

When the present king's father succeeded to the throne, the city and its folk did not fare much better. In fact, in many respects they found life to be much worse. This king was a most avaricious and mean-minded man.

He was also exceedingly vain. He increased taxes to the point where he bled his own people dry. The moderately well off became poor and the poor became destitute. The money that the king acquired was spent on himself and his palace. The only positive point to emerge from his reign was the fact that the royal palace was turned into a most lavish and beautiful piece of architecture.

A further problem was that the city walls were badly maintained which resulted in serious dilapidation. Morale amongst the city guards and the soldiery was also very low. The city was consequently often raided by bands of wandering bandit armies, thus further increasing the woes of the people.

The present king was born during the first year of his father's reign and, fortunately for himself and his people, the king, (being such an inward looking man), left the development of his son to others. To this extent the son benefited since his mother, (a most civil royal lady), provided him with an enlightened tutor who taught him all the values of civilised society. Even as a child he was beloved by all those who came into contact with him.

On his seventeenth birthday he left the court to travel and gain experience in other lands. The king did not object over much, since he was very much occupied by his own self-introspection and his own affairs and also because he was completely unaware of the worth of his son. For three years he travelled and visited other cities where he studied and acquired knowledge in the cultures and beliefs of others. He also availed himself of the knowledge of the arts, architecture and many forms of modern labouring processes.

Purity

In his twentieth year news came to him that his father had eventually killed himself in an excess of self-indulgence. He was now required to return home and succeed his father. This he did and from the first a change came over the city and its people. The first thing the new young king did was to remove the old guard and hangers-on. He gained the confidence of a group of young men and women, together with whose help he devised a new constitution for the city. The next thing he did was to use the knowledge he had gained to improve the lot of all. He invited engineers and craftsmen from abroad who improved and modernised the silver mines and the smelting works. The silversmiths he employed to teach his own subjects their craft. He employed architects to build new temples and gymnasia and he encouraged all residents to smarten up their abodes. Gardeners and landscapers were hired to beautify the parks and many gardens of the city. All this was achieved in a remarkably short time and the city became a wonder and the envy of others throughout the land.

Taxes were reduced; the land and mines were distributed amongst the people; private enterprise was encouraged; and, most of all, the people regained a pride in their city and their king and all of the subjects were ready and willing to contribute most generously in order to maintain this situation.

This then, after ten years of reign by the young king was the state of affairs. However, there was one matter which now caused the king great anxiety. This matter concerned his queen and his heir, or rather, the birth of his heir.

She sits up: Oh yes! The queen! I nearly forgot about the queen! There has got to be a queen! Tell me about her!

All right, my beauty. I will tell you about the queen.

When the king first came to the throne his mind was solely occupied with matters of politics and economics. His first duty was the improvement of the lot of his subjects and his city. Consequently, for the first five years at least, he had no time for affairs of the heart. Although there were many eligible, beautiful young women amongst his circle of friends and advisors, he viewed them only as such. It was not until the fifth year of his reign that he met and married his beloved queen.

It was at the end of the summer on a very fine day and the king and one of his young advisors were strolling in the main park. His friend reminded him of the impending harvest festival, which was to be held during the following week in the park and which was to be attended by all the people and invited dignitaries from the surrounding cities. He also reminded him of the arrival the day before the festival of an envoy, (a young princess), from the king of a nearby city. It was believed that she would be asking for economic assistance and protection for her father's city from marauding bandits. He summarily dismissed the matter from his mind.

The following week, as he sat in his chambers, the envoy was announced. The princess entered the room and the king was lost. She was tall and slender and fair as a summer's day. Her long, blonde hair fell loosely to her waist and her blue eyes were filled with stars. He immediately dismissed his advisors on the pretext that: "Since the lady is of royal descent, it appears to me a matter of prudence that our discussion should be conducted in private." With wry smiles the councillors left the chambers and the king to his devices.

Needless to say, the princess's entire request was immediately granted. During the following few days the king and the princess attended the festival together. It was obvious for all to see that the princess was as much in love with the king as he was with her. After the festival the king returned with the princess to her city where he asked her father for her hand in marriage, a request that was gladly granted since it guaranteed a strong alliance and protection. One month later, with great ceremony and celebration they were married.

For some four years after the wedding all went smoothly. The new queen was much admired and beloved by all her new subjects. She could frequently be seen out hunting with the king, or riding or just walking in the park, discoursing with every one. No man, woman or child was too humble for her attention.

In the fifth year of their marriage the queen fell pregnant, a cause for much celebration and rejoicing by the king and all around him. Her pregnancy progressed smoothly and, in the eyes of the king at least; she became even more beautiful.

Eventually there came the happy day of her confinement. The midwives and the doctors, (only the best that the city could provide), had been summoned and were in attendance. The king believed that the queen was in the best of hands and he was at peace. He was surrounded by his closest friends and in anticipation of the great event; he had a grand meal prepared on which they feasted late into the night.

She frowns: I do believe a sad event is about to take place.

Unfortunately you are right, my angel. Maybe the king has had it too good up till now. It is about time we bring some realism to our story. Nature always requires a balancing. Where there is health, there is suffering; in the midst of happiness and joy, we frequently find a measure of sadness.

I know, says she. But, there are many who invariably have fortune smile upon them. And then there are those who are able to accumulate wealth without any noticeable effort.

You are right, my precious. Indeed, there are those folk who appear to have fortune smile on them. But, we should not be fooled. It is my belief that constant fortune and wealth leads to obsession. They become so used to their good fortune that they cannot bear the fear of losing it and it is this fear which counterbalances their good fortune.

Are all obsessions dangerous?

I don't know that all obsessions are dangerous, my darling, says he. All I am sure of is that all crime is born out of obsession. What is theft if not the obsessive need to possess that which belongs to others? So is murder. Murder is the theft of someone's life in order to fulfil a certain criminal obsession.

I suppose so. But, I thought this was a fantasy. Could we not keep it nice and happy?

He smiles: No, I don't think so. A story full of joy and bliss would become terribly tedious, don't you think? If nothing bad ever happened, we would have nothing to measure the quality of the good by.

Please do not go philosophical on me now, says she. I am enjoying myself. Where do we go from here?

Ah, well now! We are coming to the birth of a princess.

It was not until late that night that the first sign of trouble manifested itself. The remains of the supper and the dishes had been cleared and most folk had retired. Only a few of the king's closest friends remained behind to keep him company. A doctor had appeared and informed the king that the queen was having some trouble with the birth, but this was nearly two hours ago and still there was no news. The king was restlessly pacing the floor. His friends were entreating him to sit down, to have a drink and to relax, but by now he was far too anxious.

It was not until sunrise that the tired and worried looking medic once again entered the king's chambers. The king, who by this time was drowsing in a comfortable chair, jumped to his feet:

"The queen! How is my queen? I want to see her! Is the child born yet?"

The medic sighed and rubbed his hands over his tired eyes: "The queen has been delivered of a beautiful princess, your majesty."

"Can I see my wife? Can I see the child?"

The medic sighed: "Yes, your majesty. But, the queen is most desperately ill. I am so sorry to be the bringer of bad tidings, your majesty, but I do not believe that the queen will live until half the day is gone."

In utmost despair the king entered the queen's chambers. The room in which she was confined was gloomy, the shutters being closed. A midwife stepped forward and placed the little newborn girl in his arms.

"Look, your majesty," whispered she. She looks just like the queen. Is she not lovely?"

The king looked down with wonder at the frailness in his arms. Then he remembered his queen and his anxiety returned. He moved to the bed:

"How do you feel, my love?"

"I am well enough," replied she. Then she waved the midwife who was tending to her away and asked her to open the shutters. The midwife protested that too much fresh air would be damaging to the health of her majesty and the baby, but the queen insisted:

"I believe that I may leave this world soon. Whether the shutters are opened or closed will make no difference to my health. Grant me the pleasure to look upon my beloved city and the sky for a final time." Then, quietly, she dismissed everybody until only the king and the babe were left.

Then the queen spoke to the king: "I know that I am about to leave this world, but I leave you this child in my stead. Unlike so many children in our society who are conceived and born by arrangement, this child was created out of love. For five brief years I have known joy and love beyond description with you. But, that will suffice. There are many that would not be as privileged as I. I look at this child and I see greatness and beauty there, as well as humility in abundance. I therefore would like to call her, Purity. My wish is that you should care for her until such time as she is old enough to take care of you. I give both of you my blessing." And, saying this, she leant back on her bed and closed her eyes and did not wake again.

Purity

She laughs: For god's sake! This is enough! You'll have me in tears in a minute! Let's have a bit of light relief!

OK! OK! I'm sorry! Where should our story go from here?

I don't know! You are constructing it.

Well, I think we should pay another visit to the oracle.

The old man sits in the atrium of the temple.

What is an atrium?

It is a sort of inner courtyard that you used to get in Roman houses. It was an open space right in the centre of the house. The roof at its centre sloped downwards on the edges and the middle was open to the sky. Underneath this chimney there was usually a pond with fish and plants.

Were there any flowers in the atrium?

Oh, I would think so, my angel. When you are better, I will build you a Roman house with an atrium.

No, my love. I will not get better. But, it is kind of you to think of me. Anyway, let us not talk of such bad things. Instead, tell me about the old man. And the temple. Did they have an atrium in temples?

Maybe not, my darling. But, who cares. It is my story and if I want my temple to have an atrium, then it will have one.

OK, then. Let's get back to the old man. What does he look like?

What do you want him to look like?

I don't know. I always think of oracles as old and grizzly looking.

Well, I think our oracle should be a bit different. Remember, he is not your run of the mill oracle. Let's say that he is dressed in a long white robe with a pair of leather sandals on his feet. He has a long, white, curly beard and long white hair. He has twinkling blue eyes. How do you like that?

Very much, thank you. Now can we continue?

Most certainly! The old man sits in the atrium of the temple, basking in the heat of the early afternoon sun. He sits on a stool in front of a low altar with a brazier on top of it. Perched on the brazier is a small pot with some boiling liquid that the oracle intermittently stirs. The bead curtains in the door of the temple rattle and the high priest appears, carrying a wrapped bundle in his arms.

The high priest bows: "I greet you, Oracle."

The oracle lies down his ladle, stands and crosses his hands on his chest: "I greet you, Holy Father."

The ceremony of the greeting dispensed with, the oracle steps round the altar, removes some objects from a stool and invites the high priest to sit down.

"What brings you here so unexpectedly, High Priest."

"I bring some good news and some very bad news, Oracle."

The oracle resumes his stirring: "Well, shall we dispense with the good news first and then bend our minds to the bad. Have you noticed, High Priest, that bad events are more often than not more than proportionate to the good events? The bad things that happen in life have a habit of obliterating that which is good. What has happened?"

"The queen has been delivered of a girl child. That is the good news."

The oracle looks up with a smile: "But, this is indeed excellent news! The gods be praised! Surely, nothing could overshadow this?"

"Ah, Oracle, I wish but that you were correct in your assumption. Unfortunately a most woeful event has taken place. I regret to say that the queen passed from us shortly after the birth."

"This is indeed terrible news! Unfortunate lady! And, more than that! Our unfortunate king! How is the king?"

"Oh, at present the king is distraught, but as you well know, he is a strong man and I have no doubt that he will bear up to this with the passing of time."

"What have you in that bundle, High Priest?"

"It is the girl child. As tradition demands, she had to be brought to the high temple to be blessed. This I have done. Now it falls to you to foretell her future and confine it to parchment which will be kept in the sacred vaults of the temple. It also falls to you to write the queen's obituary which will be placed in the tomb with her one week from now."

The oracle takes the babe from the high priest and places his hands on her head. "What will she be called?"

"She was named Purity, by the queen, before she died."

"A good name. Yes, indeed. A good name. Considering her parentage, I divine that this child will have beauty and intelligence in abundance. She may very well suffer for this, since there are many in this world who are envious of these qualities in others and who will do there utmost to be destructive. Indeed, she will have a stony path ahead of her, but I perceive that she will have the strength to endure. I will confine my observations to parchment and deliver it to you by this evening. As for my second task, that should not be too arduous. The poor lady had only been a member of our royal family for five years. Also, she had been a prudent and virtuous person whose sole contribution was to be a loving wife to the king and provide him with an heir. There is nothing that fills out an obituary as much as a few evil deeds."

The high priest smiles: "You are far too cynical, Oracle."

"I don't think so, High Priest. I am just stating the truth. Remember, "I am the truth". Just say, for example, it fell to some one to write my obituary. It would go something like this: 'He was born into the priesthood. Joined the temple at an early age. Became a priest. Eventually High Priest then, post of Oracle. Told people what they wanted to hear. Died.' Not very impressive, is it?"

The high priest grins: "You better not let those outside the temple hear you talk like this. What are you stirring in that pot?"

"Oh, it is only a potion for some gentleman's wife who has failed to conceive for these five years. My theory is that the trouble lies with him and not his wife, but this is another truth that will be unacceptable. If he spent less time in his cups, his spirit may diminish somewhat, but his flesh will definitely get stronger. Anyway, it is to work we go."

The high priest picks up the child, bows and wishes him farewell.

She smiles: I like the oracle. He is a nice man.

Yes, I think so.

Shall we continue? Shall I tell you about Purity, the child?

Oh, yes please.

The king mourned his queen for much longer than was demanded by social etiquette. For a while he was inconsolable and he retreated into himself. He stored all his emotions behind a solid wall of indifference and here he immersed himself in his grief. He lost complete interest in his social and stately duties. The running of the city was left to his councillors and advisors, but since all of them were the king's men, things went very smoothly on the whole.

In the mean time, nursemaids and servants cared for the child and it was very soon evident to all those who knew her that she was no ordinary child. As a babe she was always calm and quiet. Many believed that the child possessed most remarkable qualities. They said that, whenever the child was bathed or changed, or if any functions were performed in her presence, that her intelligent eyes would follow every movement as if she was mentally ingesting all that was done. She cried very seldom. Instead, she had an air of serenity about her and a glint in her beautiful eyes and a smile that could melt the coldest heart.

That she was possessed of a keen intellect was soon evident to those that had dealings with her. By the age of three she was fluent in her own language and by the time she reached her fourth year she was well lettered. Her tutors were of the firm belief that she would possess the knowledge of an educated adult by the time she was eight.

During her early childhood her father, (being deeply obsessed by the death of his wife), paid scant attention to his child. However, during her fourth year of life he began to take some notice of her. Time, the healer, was amply aided in its work by this child with the face of an angel. The king now began to take note of the striking resemblance of his child to his erstwhile wife. His natural inclination was towards love, affection and humour. For these many a year he had suppressed these feelings within himself, but the child struck a spark deep within him, which rapidly blossomed into a flame of benevolent emotion. At first he was only aware of her as a child, but he was soon to recognise the scope of her ability, and he took upon himself the mantle of her education. He employed the best tutors from within the city and from abroad and she received an extensive education in the arts, in the written word, philosophy, astrology and mathematics. By the time she reached her tenth year she was able to discourse with fluency on all of these.

Neither was her physical development neglected. She received training in horsemanship and hunting; she received instruction in the use of the foil and the epee; she learned to throw the javelin and to shoot with the bow and arrows. In all of these she excelled beyond her years.

She became a constant companion to the king. Like his shadow she stayed by his side and he would have it no other way. She accompanied him on the hunt and to social events. Even when he was in conference she would sit close by him and listen carefully to all that was said.

Her father also began to take a fresh interest in his duties as king. He reassembled his councillors and advisors and he once again took charge of his city.

Once his authority over the city had been re-established and its affairs put in order, he put his mind to restoring the alliance between himself and the father of his dead wife. For this purpose he dispatched an envoy to request an audience and when it was granted he foregathered himself and his entourage and went to see his father-in-law. It was here at court that he was to meet his second wife, the dark queen.

Oh! Another queen! Will she be as nice as the first queen?

I don't know. I somehow doubt it though. I think we may need some balancing.

Oh, Fiddlesticks! You and your balancing! Oh, well, it's your story. You decide.

Right, then. Let us see where the tale takes us.

The king departed for his father-in-law's city shortly after Purity's sixth birthday. They left in the early morning and arrived at their destination shortly after sunset. That evening they were royally entertained at the court of the royal palace and it was here that the king's eyes first fell on the dark lady. She was about twenty years of age and, as his first queen was as fair as a summer's day, this lady was like a starless night. Her eyes glowed like black coals and her raven hair fell to her waste. Her complexion was that of dark marble. Those that looked upon her were reminded of a deep, dark pool with countless hidden secrets. The king was most impressed by her beauty, but love for this lady did not materialise in him with the spontaneity and immediacy as it had with his fair queen.

The following day was set aside for discussions. These resulted in the forging of a new and stronger alliance between the two cities. The party remained in the city for another week and this provided ample opportunity for the king and the dark lady to become well acquainted.

She was a most remarkable lady of high intelligence and good education. She could converse and debate on most subjects and she rapidly accumulated and assimilated new ideas and thoughts. She was also an accomplished rider and every day she would accompany the king and his friends, either to the hunt or just riding through the surrounding forests for pleasure.

When the king departed for his own city, he invited his father-in-law to visit at the earliest opportunity. He also extended a private and personal invitation to the dark lady which she accepted with alacrity.

So it was that one-month from then his father-in-law and some of his courtiers, (including the dark lady), visited his city and their acquaintance were renewed. It was on this occasion that Purity and the dark lady were first introduced to each other.

Now, it has to be said that, contrary to what most believe, first impressions are not always correct. Quite often we may not like those we first meet, but with elapsing time and easing of suspicious natures a trust may often grow between parties. At other times we may be impressed by the rhetoric and demeanour of certain parties until we should discover that most of what they are is just so much hot air. However, one thing is certain: the two ladies disliked and distrusted each other most vehemently at first sight, but both being of great intellect, they kept their feelings secret from all others, especially from the king. This was on account of the fact that they both craved the love and respect of the king and would do nothing to trouble him.

Six months later the king declared that he would be married to the dark lady and a wedding date was set for the following year. The event took place just after Purity's seventh birthday and her new stepmother moved into the palace.

She stirs: I can feel trouble brewing.

You are so right, my angel.

What is going to happen next?

Purity is going to grow up and to save herself she will have to do this rather quickly.

Let's go on!

The next ten years proved to be of great significance in the life of Purity. Her educational development progressed steadily and she was soon recognised by all to be one of the most brilliant minds in the city. She also acquired a lust for knowledge of politics and by the time she was sixteen, the king gained great satisfaction in discussing affairs of state with his young daughter. Being of a firm but gentle nature she found herself to be much concerned with the fate of the poorer sections of the community and because of this she was soon adopted as their champion. As with the queen of old, she could frequently be seen walking in the park, discoursing and jibing with all.

It was not only in education that her development was discernable. In the ten years which followed she turned from a pretty child into a most beautiful woman. All who set eyes on her, (from the most humble to the most noble), fell in love with her. Gradually she acquired all the features and the poise of the fair queen. Whenever the king set eyes on her he believed that, (in appearance at least), his first love was restored to him.

Now, the ten years of Purity's adolescent development was not filled with only sweetness and light. The animosity between herself and the dark queen smouldered and grew. Purity was self-assured in her own ability and she was generous in spirit towards all those who dealt with her. On the other hand, the dark queen was very much lacking in spirit. Although she also displayed supreme confidence in her own ability, the affection shown to her stepdaughter by others caused her much jealousy and distress. She was of a most sour disposition and her natural tendency was towards distrust and suspicion of others. She became resentful, not only towards the child, but also towards the king. She would accuse him of spoiling and indulging his daughter. She was envious of the fact that he would be prepared to discuss on matters of politics with his child rather than herself. She also became resentful because she believed, (quite correctly), that the affection and loyalty of the populace was reserved for the child and not for her.

On Purity's seventeenth birthday the king decided to honour his daughter with a feast. This was to be held in the main park and all the population, from the most wealthy to the poorest, was invited. It was a most joyous occasion and all attended. The feast lasted for three days and there was more than enough for all to eat and drink. Together with the old songs, new songs were written and performed in honour of their beloved princess. New plays were performed; and, there were contests in jumping, running, jousting and falconry. And, all the time, through-out the duration of the feast, the dark queen's jealousy and resentment grew until all reason left her and she decided to take matters into her own hands.

Oh, dear! I hope she is not going to do something too rash!

I think she may very well, my love. You see, obsession is rearing its ugly head again.

Is jealousy of others the same as obsession?

Oh, I believe so. Jealousy is the obsessive need to possess something's that others have, weather physical, mental, characteristic or material. And, as we shall see shortly, our beloved queen also has an obsession with power.

What is she going to do?

Let's just say that, those who become obsessed with the domination of others will stoop to any means to reach their objective. Anyway, let us briefly return to the temple and observe some events.

✠

The bead curtains rattle and the old man looks up. Although the expression on his face does not change, he is overcome by a feeling of amazement. The dark queen stands in the doorway. Since he very seldom leaves these temple walls and she has had no occasion to visit him, he has never met her, but he knows her from what others have told him. She bows:

"I greet you, Oracle."

The oracle speaks: "I am what was; I am the here and now; I am the future; I am the truth; I am the mirror of my people; I am the oracle; I greet you."

The oracle indicates the vacant stool opposite him. "Is there anyway in which I can be of assistance to your majesty?"

She sits down: "I don't know, oracle. Maybe it is just time for me to visit all my subjects and find out what they are up to."

He notes with interest the words, "my subjects". "Rather presumptuous," he thinks. "At least it should be "the king's subjects", at most, "our subjects". Since when has she acquired the mantle of ruler of the people?" Like the child so many years ago, he has an immediate dislike of the queen. He says nothing.

She looks at the holy man before her and she knew him on the instant for what he was: her adversary. Although respectful and courteous, he lacks reverence. She also notes that he did not bow to her, neither physically nor in spirit and her dark heart fills with ire.

She continues: "Tell me, Oracle – I am interested in your greeting. What exactly does it mean? For example, you say: "I am what was; I am the here and now; I am the future;" Let's start with that. What does that mean?"

"It means that I keep a record of past events, that I am aware of current affairs and if I use the data from these that I am in a position, to a certain extent, to be able to predict the future."

"Well then. What about, "I am the truth"? Do you always tell the truth?

"I some times advise folk that the truth may not be very palatable. But, if they insist on hearing it, I will tell it."

"What about, "I am the mirror of my people"? What do you mean by that?"

"I reflect the feelings of the people.

"Not their wishes?"

"No, your majesty. That is the domain of the king."

"Right then, Oracle. I wish to hear the truth. What are the feelings of the people?"

"In respect of what, your majesty?"

"In respect of the royal family, for instance. What do they think of the king, his daughter and myself?"

"I extend to you the same warning as I do to others – you may not like the truth."

"Don't worry, Oracle. I crave the truth."

"Well then, your majesty. It is thus: The king is revered by the people as a kind and just man. For more than twenty years now the city has existed in peace and prosperity. This is due to our king and the people love him for that. As for his daughter, she has found a way to their hearts and as they loved and idolised her mother, so they love and idolise the child."

"Then, what about me, Oracle? What do they think of me?"

"They afford you the courtesy which you deserve as the king's wife, your majesty."

"Thank you, Oracle. That is all I wanted to hear."

She stands and leaves. He scratches his head in contemplation. "Now, what was all that about? What ever it was, I don't believe I like it very much. This will need much careful thought and even more careful handling."

I really don't like her very much!

You're not supposed to, my darling.

Is she going to do something evil?

Well, let's put it like this: The king and his daughter will have to be very careful. Let's continue.

※

It was in the early springtime that the king first began to feel unwell. He felt devoid of energy and he had no strength to perform his daily tasks.

He also had no desire to devote himself to those things which used to give him pleasure. The queen blamed it on inadequate nutrition and from then on she took it upon herself to personally prepare and serve his food. She also put her personal physician, (a man who she trusted implicitly), at his disposal.

But, in spite of all this the king's health was in rapid decline. After some time he was afflicted by nausea, stomach cramps and agonising pains in his extremities. At night he would pace the floor, unable to sleep because of the pain. He became drawn and tired and his once sturdy physique became fleshless. The king's councillors and advisors implored his wife to allow the eminent physicians of the city to attend to her husband, but she ignored their requests. She insisted that this would cast a slur on the character and ability of her own physician. The consequences of this were that his deterioration progressed with swift inevitability.

Finally, there came a day when the king was unable to rise from his bed. Now, even the services of the queen's physician were dispensed with. For two days she personally tended to him, never leaving his side. In the appearance of her devotion to her husband, at least, none could find any just cause to criticise her.

After the king had taken to his bed, he would frequently summon his daughter to come and talk to him. He had a foreboding that he would never rise again. For long hours he would discourse on the history of the city: his grandfather, his father and the fair queen, her mother whom she had never known. He would also talk about the future and he urged her to be kind, generous and just to her people. But, even in this matter of communion between father and daughter the dark queen interfered. She urged the king to rest and eventually she forbid Purity's visits.

Then, on the third day after he had taken to his bed, the king died. The city went into mourning. Quite often the people would mourn for the loss of a person, because tradition demands that it should be so. But, on this occasion their grief was sincere. All the folk of the city loved their king.

Oh, dear! Two down! How many to go? I hope you are not going to kill all the nice people off!

I'll try not to do that. But, you know, the oracle was right. Just as a life with a bit of evil makes for a more interesting obituary, so a good story requires some unpleasantness in order to keep the attention of the listeners. You would not want me to bore you with a story that is only full of sweetness and light, would you, my darling?

No, I suppose not. Go on then! What happens next?

***

The high priest enters the courtyard: "Have you heard?"

The oracle nods, "Yes. It is indeed tragic news. On this occasion I will perform my functions with a heavy heart. Where is the king's body now?"

"With the embalmers. As you know, they have to prepare the body. After embalming they will wrap him in anointed cloth from head to foot in order to preserve him for the life here after. They will be the last ones in this world of the living to see his face. The next stop on his journey will be when he reaches the domain of the gods. All that remains for me to do now is to go and bestow my final blessing before the body is covered."

"Has the body been inspected by any of the city physicians?"

"No. This has been done by the queen's physician. He made the declaration of death."

The oracle looks up with a far away gleam in his eyes: "Holy Father. May I make a request of you?"

"Of course you may."

Purity

The oracle makes his request.

The high priest frowns: "What you ask for is most unusual. Are you sure that such action is necessary?"

"I think so, Father. At least, if I don't find anything, we will have peace of mind."

"And, if you should discover anything? Then, what do we do?"

"I really could not say, Holy Father. I have no idea. Maybe the gods will give us guidance. But, you know? Somehow I believe that we will be left to our own devices. Over the years I have perceived that, when necessity calls, the gods are remarkably lacking in direct action."

The high priest chuckles: "You know, Oracle. Do not ever mention this to anyone, but I tend to agree with you. Only because, if the gods were powerful, they would long since have struck you down for your lack of reverence."

He leaves the courtyard.

✵

The priest enters the room. He wears a cloak and a veil. He carries a bowl of water and over his shoulder is draped a linen cloth. In the middle of the room stands a plinth with some figures around it. They are the embalmers. On the plinth there is the outline of a body, covered in sheets. On the walls of the room can be seen row upon row of shelves containing jars and bottles of ointments and embalming fluids, as well as rolls of cloth.

The priest gestures to the figures around the plinth and they leave the room. He steps up to the plinth and removes the sheet covering the body. He pulls the hair back from the forehead and washes and dries the face. Then he performs the same task with the hands and feet. And, all the while in a low voice, he requests from the gods entrance into the afterlife for this departed soul.

After the ceremony had been completed, he once again covers the body with the white sheet. He smoothes down the sheet and picks up the holy water and leaves the room.

The high priest enters the courtyard: "It was indeed a strange request you made of me. But, I have known you for a long time and I know that you would not ask for such a thing lightly. We all know that you should not leave the temple grounds unless circumstances utterly demand it. You have always taken your duties as oracle seriously, although it has to be said, not very reverentially. Now, can you tell me: Why did you want to see the body?"

"I don't rightly know. Let us just say that I find it most peculiar that a man who was full of health and vigour should decline so swiftly. I thought that, maybe by looking at the body I may get an inkling into the cause of his death."

"I thought so. I have to say I am of the same mind as you. Now, tell me. Did you find anything?"

"I am afraid so. I examined the skin and eyes as well as the nails and hair and there is no doubt in my mind that the king had been poisoned."

"As you suspected. I was hoping that you might be wrong. So, what do you suggest we do about it?"

"There is not much we can do. I suggest that we wait and see. I have always found that those who dabble with evil eventually succumb to it."

She sits up and stretches: Well, well! This is getting exciting! So, the queen murdered the king!

Oh, yes. I think we can safely assume that.

What is she going to do next?

I think she may try and take control of the city. You see, those who are consumed with a lust for something tend to start quite slowly with their mischief. They test the water, so to speak. The killing of the king was her first step. Now that she knows that she can get away with murder, it is safe to assume that further action on her part will be swift and that her deeds will be more daring.

And, what about Purity?

You will have to wait and see.

Well, come along then! Let's hear what's going to happen!

For a while the queen went into mourning, but it did not last for very long. She considered it to be a waste of time better spent on fulfilling her ambitions. However, she did use the time of mourning to devise and perfect her plans for the future.

Now, we need to know exactly what the queen desired before we could possibly understand her needs to act in this most bizarre and evil manner. She possibly would have been reasonable in her actions if those around her had been affectionate towards her. But, when she realised that none loved her, a great jealousy grew within her which in time grew into an obsession; an obsession that grew into a sickness; an obsession to dominate all and, if necessary, to destroy all those that may stand in her way.

Her ultimate aim was to sit on the throne and to wear the crown. To this end she set her plans in motion to re-organise and restructure the political system of the city.

It so happens that a number of her friends from her previous home lived in the city; friends that she had invited when she married the king. Now, during her time of mourning, she sent these friends back to her home city with instructions to bring back as many of her admirers as they could persuade. On return all these followers were installed, either in the palace or in spacious accommodation surrounding the palace.

In this city, on the death of a king, succession to the throne took place thus: If there were a number of children, the oldest son would be the heir to the throne. If there were no sons the oldest daughter would succeed. The heir could not succeed to the throne until he or she became of age at eighteen. If there were no children, the queen would become the next monarch. But, if there were a child in line for the throne, the queen would act as consort until such time as he or she reached their eighteenth birthday.

Purity was to be installed as queen on her eighteenth birthday, six months hence. The reason for curtailing her mourning was because the dark queen had so little time at her disposal. Her first action was to disband most of the old set of councillors and advisors and to put her own followers in their stead. She let it be known that she was only interested in modernising the system. As a token, therefore, she left in place a few of the deceased king's councillors. She also removed the palace guard and replaced them with men loyal to herself. Finally, she re-organised the city guards and the soldiery. All the influential positions in these disciplines were filled with her own followers. From the surrounding lands she recruited thousands of mercenaries. To these men she promised great wealth in return for their loyal support. Everything was now in place for her to take total control. All that was needed was to dispose of Purity.

She sighs: I suppose that was inevitable.

Yes, my love. I'm afraid so.

But, didn't Purity know what was going on? Didn't she do anything to stop it?

No. She could not. Remember, she was only seventeen. And, apart from that, being of such a kind and trusting nature I would doubt that it ever crossed her mind that any person could have such evil intent towards herself.

Oh, well. I suppose it's got to happen then. How is she going to do it?

I will tell you.

※

In that city lived a hunter. He was unlike any other man of the population.

He was solitary and aloof and he kept his own council. He showed allegiance to no one. His time was spent hunting on the planes below the city or wandering and exploring the depths of the dark forest.

During those isolated periods when he did stay in the city he lived by himself in a small abode near the west wall. Here he lived a frugal life. His existence was meagre. He asked for nothing from others and he provided no assistance to any.

His only pride was in his own skills as a hunter and the trophies that bedecked his walls. These were many and varied, consisting of the heads, horns and skins of deer and other wild animals. Pride of place went to the head of a silver tiger that was suspended above his front door. Slung on hooks along the walls amongst his trophies, were his hunting equipment, consisting of bows and arrows, spears and snares and many other weapons, the use of which was only known to him.

Most folk held him in awe, because of his alleged adventures. It was well known that he had slain a silver tiger, an animal that very few had ever encountered. It was also rumoured that he had travelled further than any other person in the city. Evidence of this was found in the fact that he could converse freely with those strangers in their own languages who visited the city from the other side of the dark forest. These men came to trade and, when he was at home, the hunter was employed to act as interpreter in the market place.

Although a solitary man, the hunter was not immune to the intrigues of the city. He kept his ear close to the ground and he was aware of the strange circumstances of the king's demise. He also noted the discord that existed between the queen and the princess. But, the hunter kept himself aloof from these events. It was his belief that his survival as a hunter and as a person depended on his single-minded pursuit of his own ambitions. His attitude towards other folk could not even be described as ambivalent. In fact, he considered himself to have no emotional attachment towards others. In the animal kingdom he was a hunter and amongst people he was perceived as nothing more than a mercenary.

Being aware of his lack of loyalty to others and also knowing that his services could be bought, the queen now turned to this man for help in the furtherance of her plans.

What is she going to do?

Be patient, my angel. I am going to tell you.

※

One evening, when the queen knew that the hunter was at home, she went to visit him. Because she did not want others to know of her errand, she took some precautions. First, she went under cover of darkness when she knew that very few would be abroad in the palace grounds or the city streets. She also made sure that she should not be recognised by any that may see her. She dressed herself in servant's clothes and covered her head and face with a veil. It was in this manner that she approached the house of the hunter.

He was at his evening meal when there came a knock at the door. He was not over pleased with this intrusion into his solitude and with a disgruntled air he moved to the door and unlatched it.

In front of him stood a serving girl, her head and face covered with a veil.

"What is this? Why am I to be disturbed at this late hour?"

"May I come in, Master? I am sent here by the queen to make a request of you."

He was immediately beset by suspicion. This girl did not have the speech of the everyday servant. Her voice was modulated and her accent was most refined. His curiosity got the better of him and the hunter opened the door wide and beckoned her into the room. He indicated a seat, but the maid remained standing. Then, she lifted her veil and the hunter recognised her with a start.

"Now, why would the dark queen visit me at this time of the day and why would she attire herself in this strange manner?"

"Let me come straight to the point, Hunter, and let me not waste the time of either of us. I wish you to grant me a favour."

"With respect, your majesty: I am not in the business of doing favours for others."

"Are you then in a position to refuse me, Hunter?"

"Maybe not, your majesty. But, I have learnt that it is very dangerous to extract favours from those who are unwilling to grant them. They will do all in their power to renege and to release themselves from an unwelcome obligation."

"Then, tell me: Will you perform a task for me; A task for which you will receive ample remuneration?"

"Now, that is more to my liking! What is this task you wish me to perform?"

"When you go hunting next I would like the king's daughter to accompany you."

"Not too much of a task, your majesty. I have to admit that she will be a nuisance since I like only my own company when travelling, but if the price is right I am sure that I could cope with this small inconvenience."

"That is not all, Hunter. I wish the girl to have an accident in the forest. She must never appear in this city again."

The hunter looked startled: "You would like me to kill her?"

"Yes."

"She is well-beloved by all the dead kings subjects. Since she would be in my care, I will be held responsible for her death."

"I will pay you well, Hunter."

"This act will indeed demand a great sum."

"How much?"

"Let us say – 100,000 gold pieces."

"That is a fair sum, Hunter. You will receive half the money before you leave and the rest on your return without the girl. But, I insist that you provide me with some evidence of her demise."

"That shall be done."

"When will you leave?"

"One week from now."

"Good. That will give me time to persuade the girl to accompany you."

She moved to the door, wished the hunter a goodnight and disappeared into the dark.

After she had gone, the hunter returned to his seat in front of the fire and immersed himself in contemplation of the circumstances that had so unexpectedly been thrust upon him. Although he had no regards for others, he was fully aware of the love and esteem which the people of the city extended to their princess. He realised that, if it should ever be discovered that he had a hand in her death, he would never again find safe haven amongst these folk. On the other hand, he knew the queen for what she was: a ruthless and ambitious woman. Maybe he recognised some of himself in her. He soothed his troubled conscience by persuading himself that he had no choice in this matter. The lure of the money was also great and after some time he resigned himself to his future actions with a relatively untroubled spirit.

She is really evil, isn't she? Will she stop at nothing?

She is ambitious, Darling. She is also ruthless.

"But, surely. The hunter cannot be so heartless?

Maybe he cannot, maybe he can. We will have to see where the story takes us.

On the following night the queen casually expressed the view that Purity needed to improve her hunting skills, a view that the princess heartily concurred with. The queen also said that a break from her normal surrounds would do her some good. Since her father's death she had been in constant mourning and the queen suggested that the hunting trip should act as a diversion. The king's councillors, however, expressed their reservations:

"In our opinion she already spends enough time outside the city walls. She is always in the company of soldiers and hunters. We don't see much of her in the palace as it is. And, anyway, who is there that could teach her more than she knows already?"

"Why not ask the Hunter?" suggested the queen.

Once again the councillors were uncertain: "He is a strange man who likes his own company."

"That he is, indeed," Replied the queen. But, there is no harm in asking him. Above all, I believe that he has sufficient knowledge of the wild to ensure her safety."

At last Purity (who was most anxious for this plan to come to fruition), and the queen persuaded them to approach the hunter with a request that he should take the princess with him on his subsequent expedition. A member of the council was forthwith dispatched and the hunter readily complied with his request. A week later they left the city. The hunt was to last for two weeks.

The first three days they spent roaming the planes at the foot of the hills on which the city stood. Here the hunter taught her the various skills that were needed to hunt successfully in the open. He taught her how to track an animal; he taught her how to stalk a deer; he showed her how to camouflage herself in the open; he taught her how to set a fire so that it may burn through-out the night and he showed her how to strike a camp. He imparted to her the knowledge to interpret the signs of nature; in short, he taught her all he knew and he was eminently impressed with her thirst for knowledge and the swiftness with which she grasped and absorbed all she was told.

Somewhat to his annoyance he found himself to be drawn in a strange manner to this young girl in a way that he had never before been attracted to any other human being. On leaving the city, he believed that she would be a hindrance and an encumbrance to him, but he was soon to change his mind. He found her quick and eager to learn, most skilful with bow and spear and the setting of snares and, above all, she possessed a quiet assurance in her own ability. Soon he found himself to be discoursing with her in a manner most alien to his nature. He told her about his life, his adventures and his travels to foreign lands and he told her about the strange and wonderful sights he encountered. By the third day, when they entered the forest, there was a strong bond between the two of them and he began to have serious misgivings about the unpleasant task ahead of him.

For three further days they wandered through the forest where he taught her how to find her way north, south, west and east, how to recognise the edible fruits and roots of the forest and how to hunt animals in areas where bows and arrows were of little use. It was on the fourth day that he braced himself to perform the act.

Purity had left him for a short while to collect water from a nearby spring and he had decided to kill her on her return. His choice of weapon was the bow and arrow. As she entered the clearing where they were encamped, he would shoot her through the heart. He considered himself to be an expert marksman and he was sure that she would not suffer much.

Soon he heard her returning. She was singing and her voice was as clear as a bell. Now, the hunter who was by this time experiencing the most severe pangs of conscience, was most unwilling to let her see his face whilst performing the act. He therefore hid himself behind a tree and waited for her to approach. She entered the clearing with a flask of water in her hands. He took aim and let loose his arrow. At that precise moment she caught her foot on a tree root and pitched forwards onto the ground, spilling the water as she fell. The arrow flew harmlessly over her head and disappeared into the branches behind her. The princess, (being so disturbed by her fall), was totally unaware of the arrow that passed so close by her. The hunter found himself strangely relieved by what had happened. He took this to be a sign that the deed was not to be done. He rushed from his hiding place and picked her up from where she had fallen, being most solicitous.

That night after they had consumed their evening meal and Purity had retired, he sat alone and thought about what was to be done. If he returned with the princess, he had no doubt that the queen would have him killed. He had recognised in her the obsession which drove her. Alternatively he could flee and not return to the city, but this was not to his liking. He was a man who did not take kindly to having his actions decided for him. He therefore plumbed for a third option: He would leave the girl here alive and return, claiming that he had slain her. But, what ever was to be done, he would have to tell her the truth and about the danger that she would encounter if she should return.

Early the next morning he woke her from her slumbers and after they had broken their fast, he told her all. Purity was appalled by the evil that was to befall her, but, being endowed with a most generous nature, she forgave the hunter his part in these deeds. She agreed with him that she could not return. They consequently devised a plan of further action.

They would stay together for another week, during which time the hunter would escort her as far as he could to the other side of the forest. During this time they would accumulate sufficient provisions for her to complete her journey. He suggested that she should make her way to a place he knew, the land of the canyon dwellers. Here lived a most civil race and he believed that she would be safe in their midst.

On the last day of their travels he provided her with weapons and food and directions to the land of the canyon dwellers. Before he bid her farewell he spoke to her and said:

"The queen will want some proof that I have slain you. Do you possess anything which I may take with me as a token?

Purity thought for a while and then replied: "Around my neck I wear a golden chain on which is suspended a gold nugget in the shape of a heart. This was left to me by my mother and never in all my seventeen summers have I removed it from my person. Furthermore, on your way back to the city, you should hunt down a bore or a deer or some other animal and remove its heart. If you present the queen with these two objects, I am certain that she would accept this as proof of my demise. Remember that she has so much faith in her own ruthlessness and the fear she inspires in others that she will not expect you to renege on her."

Saying so, she removed the chain from her neck and handed it to the hunter. He then bid her farewell and, with a heavy heart, he left her to fend for herself.

Well, at least the hunter turned out to be a good man, didn't he?

Yes, my love.

Will anything bad happen to him?

I don't know yet, my angel. I haven't thought that far yet. We will just have to see where the story takes us.

But, what is Purity going to do now? She is all alone!

I know, but I am sure she will survive. Let's see.

✠

And, so she sat alone, her back braced against a tree. Around her were scattered her meagre belongings: the tools of her new trade, (a hunter of animals), some provisions and a few articles of clothing. Once she was part of an elite community in which she lived in bounty and protection. All she needed in life was at her disposal: there were servants to see to her every need; never had she wanted for food or clothing; her every wish for comfort, (however big or small), would be fulfilled; and, most of all, she longed for the love and protection of her kinsmen and her people.

Thus she sat, contemplating her lot in utter despair. But, she was a resourceful girl and she was not prone to feeling sorry for herself. Soon her mind veered away from self-pity and she began to review her situation in a positive light. Over the years, (and lately, especially with the help of the hunter), she had acquired a great deal of knowledge and she was certain that she could give a good account of herself in the wild. The land about her contained ample stores of food and she was sure that she would not starve.

She also had youth on her side and soon the natural confidence of the young asserted itself. Her despair left her and it was soon replaced with a feeling of excitement. Her father was dead and most of the councillors, (who were also her friends), were now replaced by the queen's friends. So, from that point of view there was not much for her to go back to. This was also a good chance for her to travel the world and to visit foreign lands and meet their inhabitants. So, instead of brooding on her misfortune, she considered it a godsend opportunity for her to quench her thirst for knowledge. She only had to be careful in the wilderness. She knew that there would be many unforeseen dangers in front of her, but she had ample faith in her own abilities and resourcefulness. So, it was with a much lighter spirit that she viewed her future.

It was now late afternoon and the light of the day was fading fast. She rose from where she sat and collected some water from a nearby spring. She then build and lit a fire on which she prepared her evening meal. Then she rolled herself in a blanket and went to sleep.

Is she going to cope? Will she survive?

I sincerely hope so, my love. If she doesn't it will bring our story to a rather premature end and we couldn't have that now, could we, my angel?

I suppose so. But, I'll tell you what; there is an awful lot of angst in this story and it is beginning to do my head in. I suggest we have a little rest.

Part 2: Wilderness

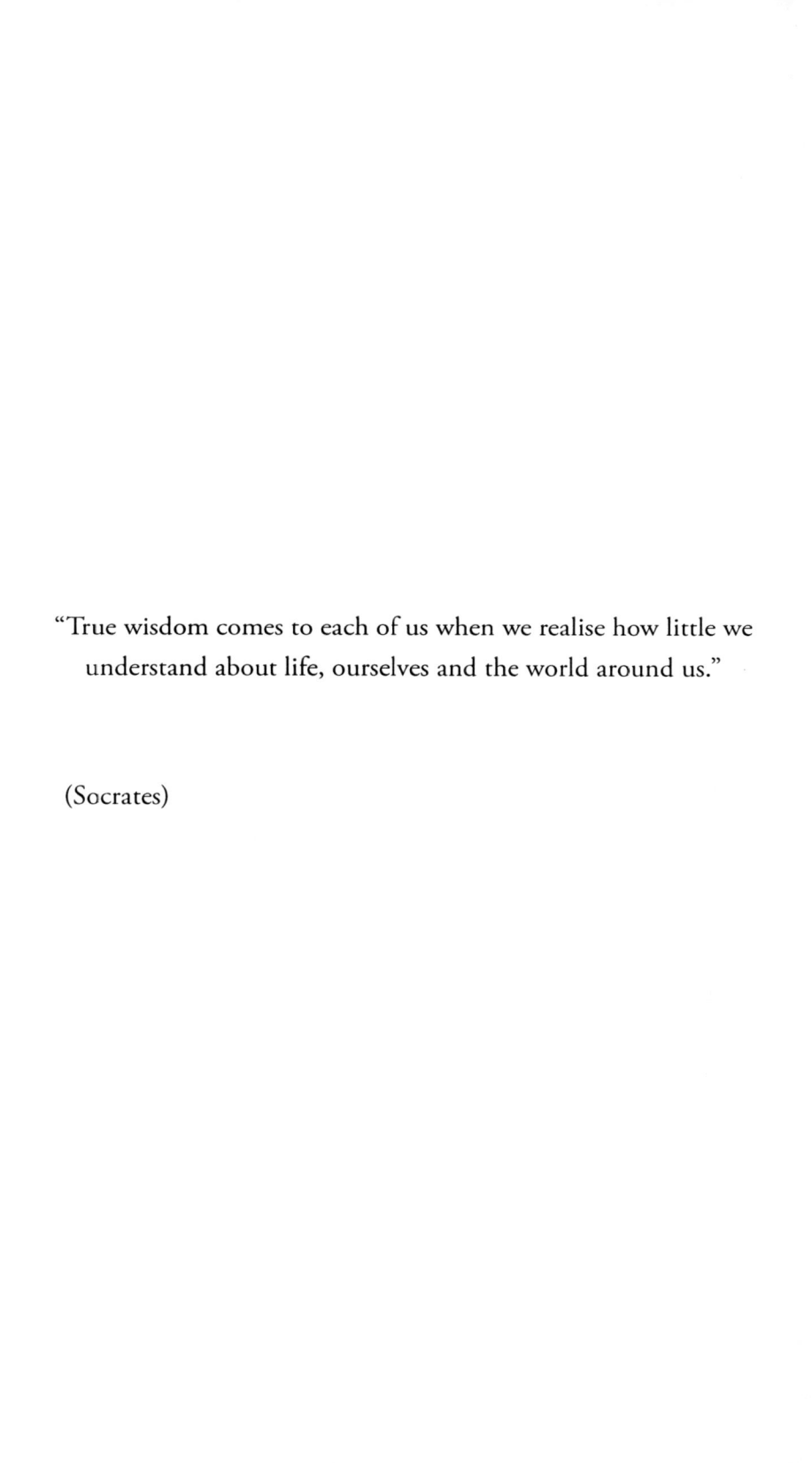

"True wisdom comes to each of us when we realise how little we understand about life, ourselves and the world around us."

(Socrates)

SHALL WE CONTINUE?

Yes, my angel.

How about a précis?

Why not? Let's see, what has happened so far? We have met the oracle who is rather sceptical of others' perception of truth and honesty. However, unconventional as he is, he is quite prepared to step outside the bounds of his own profession to elicit truths as he perceives them.

Our story is set in a mythical city which is very prosperous, due to the silver mines from the surrounding mountains. The people of the city had not always been wealthy. During the present king's grandfather's and father's reigns the mines had been allowed to fall into disrepair, but now, due to the new king's enlightened efforts, wealth and happiness had returned to the people.

The king rules over the city and he guides his people to prosperity and contentment. He marries the fair queen who bears him a girl-child, but she dies in childbirth. It is soon realised that the young princess possesses exceptional intelligence and she is well educated in all the sciences as well as outdoor activities, such as fencing, hunting and horsemanship.

After some time the king marries the dark queen who rapidly finds herself in emotional conflict with the king and the child. As is the case with the king and his daughter, she wishes to be loved and revered by the people. Instead, all she receives is the respect due to her as the king's wife. She is beset by an all-consuming jealousy, which eventually results in her murdering the king. This foul deed is uncovered by the oracle, but in view of the power of the queen, he decides to remain quiet.

The queen replaces all the king's old advisors with her own councillors and finally she decides to rid herself of the princess. To this purpose she approaches the hunter, a solitary and mercenary man who shows no allegiance to anybody. After offering him a handsome bribe, she instructs the hunter to take the young girl on a hunt into the forest where he is to dispose of her, bringing back a token to show that the deed had been successfully completed.

The hunter does as he is bid, but during their travels he befriends the young princess and when the time arrives, he is unable to kill her. He informs the princess as to the fate that was to befall her and he advises her not to return to the city, but to travel to the land of the Canyon-Dwellers where she would be safe.

She presents him with a jewel, a golden heart on a chain that was given to her by her dead mother and had never left her person since her birth. She also advises him to kill some wild animal and to present the jewel and the animal's heart to the queen. She was certain that the queen would accept these as tokens of her demise. The hunter returns to the city and the princess is left alone in the forest to fend for herself. Will that do, my angel?

Yes, I think so. But, can we pause for a while and examine our characters in more detail. You see, I know this is a fantasy, but I would like to believe in them. At present I find them to be too black and white. The king and the dark queen, for example, are respectively just too good and to evil to be true.

Fair enough. Who shall we start with?

The king. Do you not think that the king should have had some weaknesses?

He very likely did. Remember, he was ultimately a politician. You know that, in our country, the insane are not allowed to stand for parliament. In my opinion, anyone who feels the need to be a politician should be treated in the same way. I believe that those who have a burning desire to be politicians must be slightly mad. I am also cynical enough to believe that most "professional" politicians eventually sacrifice the hopes of the people in favour of their own egotistical self-interest. But, our king, on the other hand, was born into politics. So he had little choice in the matter. But, he surrounded himself with advisors. Maybe the advice was not always of the best, but this is fortunately not a political story, so we may as well draw a veil over this. Anyway, in this tale he had a weakness: he married the dark queen which proved to be his undoing. The dark queen, on the other hand, was obviously a megalomaniac and we might as well leave it at that. As far as the oracle is concerned, I have never met one which fortunately relieves me from the necessity to comment on his character.

What about the hunter? He seems to be a rather complex person.

Ah, The hunter, indeed. You are right, my precious. We will discuss his character at a later stage. For now, let us follow him back to the city.

✠

It was late afternoon when the hunter returned to the city. The guards at the gates saw him coming from a long way off and they noted that he was travelling alone. They made haste to inform the queen of the fact that Purity was not in the company of the hunter. The queen, wishing to make a public display of the death of the princess, prepared herself in a hurry and, assuming a sombre countenance full of anxiety, she made her way to the city gates where she confronted the hunter.

"Good day to you, Hunter. How was your journey?

"Oh, your majesty! Some event has taken place that has indeed overshadowed all else!"

"What has happened, Hunter? And, what has become of the princess?"

"It is the fate of the princess that concerns me. I am distraught with grief over that which had befallen her."

"What is this, Hunter? Tell it all."

"We spent three days on the planes below the city before we entered the forest. During this time I taught her many skills and she conducted herself well. We spent some time in the forest and it was here, on the seventh evening, that tragedy struck. The princess went to a nearby spring to collect some water. In the distance I heard a great roaring and screams and I made haste to her aid. When I reached the spring I perceived a great silver tiger that was savaging the princess. I managed to chase the beast away, but, alas, I was too late. The princess had been severely mauled and she was dead. I buried her where she had fallen and, as a token of her demise, I brought you this jewel that she carried permanently on her person." And since her body was so badly mauled by the animal, I removed only her heart so that it could be entombed amongst her own people. Saying this he extended to her the golden heart on its chain as well as a wooden box containing the heart of the slaughtered boar.

Then, the queen, in mock despair raised her hands and covered her face and mourned for her stepdaughter. Soon the wailing was taken up by those nearby and the news of the death of the princess spread like wild fire throughout the city. At least the grieving amongst the king's folk was genuine.

The queen immediately called for a period of mourning and all the city folk complied. The doors and windows of the houses were covered in black drapes and all went about their business in quiet solitude.

But, mingled with the grief for the death of the princess was fear; a fear that was so awesome in it's contemplating that few wished to express it aloud. Rumours concerning the king's death and the queen's hand in this matter were spreading amongst the people. Also, she was now the sole heir to the throne and many had noted the changes to the council and the palace guard. The checks on the queen that were provided by the king and the princess were now removed. The queen was now widely distrusted and all feared for the future and safety of their city.

Why did they not rise up and overthrow her?

That would not have been so easy, my angel. You must understand that in this world there are millions of followers and very few leaders. That is how it has to be. If you had as many leaders as followers it would lead to endless conflict and confusion. All the queen had to do was to remove all the leaders of the people. She had already started on this road by removing the king's council and the city and palace guards. Now, any one that spoke against her or that she suspected of disloyalty was either imprisoned or executed under a trumped-up charge of treason or some other vague crime.

And, what happened to the hunter?

Oh, he received his ill-gained money and disappeared once more into obscure solitude.

Will he get away with it?

We'll have to see, my darling. We'll have to see. In the mean time I think we should make another visit to the oracle.

―

The high priest and the oracle are sitting in the courtyard of the temple.

"Have you heard the news, Oracle?"

"I have indeed, Holy Father."

"And, what are your thoughts?"

"My thoughts are rather disturbed, High Priest."

"Will you share them with me?"

"Most certainly, Holy One. Speaking them aloud may help to clear my mind and I may have a better view of things."

"Well, let's make a start then. What is it that concerns you?"

"Well, High Priest, it has to do with coincidences. I do not trust them. In my experience coincidences are quite often manufactured in order to hide some other misdemeanour."

"And, what pray, are these coincidences that concern you so, Oracle?"

"Well, we have the death of a king, followed by the death of a princess. Both you and I now know that the king's death was achieved by foul means. Just preceding these two events I was visited by the queen who extensively quizzed me on her standing with the people. She made me feel as if I was a judge at a popularity contest. And now our princess has died, only a matter of months before her accession to the throne. Since I suspect our queen of high ambition I would say that all these events fit far too neatly into her plans. To coin an ancient phrase High Priest, all this has the smell of a tramp's undergarments."

"So, what do you propose we do, Oracle?"

"There is nothing we can do, Holy One, but to sit and wait. An unharassed hare will ever gain in confidence and eventually snare himself."

"These are indeed troubling times, Oracle. I am told that there are many strange folk entering the city. The new guards are not as careful as the old. Apparently, bandits, vagrants and other foreigners are within our city walls. There is an increase in lawlessness in the streets and in the market place. I tell you, Oracle, I fear for our city."

The high priest rises from his seat with a sigh and leaves the courtyard.

Why does the oracle not do something about the queen?

As he says, my angel. There is not a lot that he can do.

What is going to happen next?

I think we need to have a look and see how Purity is getting on, don't you think?

Yes. I think you are right.

※

Before leaving the forest, Purity had stumbled upon a wide track that was obviously used by humans and animals alike. She had left the forest by this track and she had entered a terrain of undulating hills and grassy vales. In the distance she could see a range of low mountains that stretched from west to east as far as the eye could see. It was towards these mountains that she made her way.

Although she had met no one up till the present, she realised that the country she was in was well attended, since the many tracks she came upon were covered in the footprints of human travellers. For her own safety's sake she decided to avoid human contact as far as possible and she therefore proceeded with the utmost caution. To this purpose she had coiled her long blonde hair in a tight knot on her head and covered it with a veil of linen. In a land that she presumed would be inhabited mainly by male travellers, she judged that it would be most unwise for her to be spotted and recognised as a vulnerable female. To this purpose she donned herself in her riding gear of breeches, high boots and a baggy shirt. To all intents and purposes she now appeared as a young male.

It was on the second night after she had entered the land of hills that she encountered the first human since the hunter had left her.

All day she had been aimlessly following the many paths that stretched between the hills. On reaching a crossroad she would take either a left or a right path on a whim and follow the next path until the same. Since she had nowhere to go in the first place she did not consider herself lost. It was a beautiful warm day and she enjoyed the aspect of the country she was travelling through. In the early evening she came across a small copse by the side of the path she was following. On entering the copse she found a small clearing and she decided to make her camp for the night on this spot.

After fetching some water in a pitcher, she struck a fire and proceeded to roast a hare that she had snared earlier in the day. She had removed the linen cloth from her head and untied her hair, allowing it to fall loosely to her waist. She had also removed her travel-stained boots and breeches and she was now wearing a loose linen cloak.

Thus she was, taking her ease, when she heard a small rustling behind her. She turned her head and saw, standing no more than two arms lengths from her, a rustic looking man. His features were contorted with a most malevolent grin.

"So, what 'ave we got 'ere? A wench! And, if me eyes is not deceivin' me, not just any old hag! A most ansome wench indeed! And, some food cookin' and all! I must say: the gods around 'ere knows 'ow to provide for the weary traveller! I'll tell you what, darlin': My body is sendin' me brains some very pleasant messages! It is tellin' me that I am regular famished, both for wenches and for roastin' 'ares! I thinks I might 'ave the wench first and then I may let 'er share the little old 'are with me for dessert!"

Now, the rustic already had made two mistakes: his first mistake was to under-estimate her, because he thought of her as a mere girl. His second mistake was to blabber at her for too long. This gave her a chance to recover from her surprise at seeing him so close to her and to prepare herself for his assault. In her mind she heard the voice of the hunter: "If ever you should be confronted by a dangerous wild animal, just keep your eyes on his. From his eyes you will gather when he is going to jump at you and this will allow you to take appropriate action."

This, then, is what she did as he strode towards her and she noted that his eyes were filled with a mixture of mirth and lust. She realised that he thought of her as a ripe peach that could be plucked with the minimum of effort. It was time to disillusion him of this fact. As he reached for her, she ducked under his arm and, snatching the short dagger that was permanently strapped to the outside of her lower leg, she struck upwards with the speed of a snake and buried the blade in the soft flesh above his wrist. At the same time she ducked sideways from under his outstretched arms and plucked the knife from his forearm.

He roared like a wounded bull and turned to face her. "I see the wench has got talons! In my way of thinkin' she needs to be taught a lesson."

Once again Purity kept her eyes on his. The look of astonishment when she stabbed him had now changed to one of cold fury. He began to stalk her and she moved backwards in a circle until she was between him and the fire.

"Oh, dearie, dearie me," Said he. "Me thinks the little wench is trapped! "If she steps any farther back she will burn her lovely little arse! Now, to my way of thinkin', that will be a real shame!"

She noted from the expression in his eyes that he was going to make another grab for her. As he launched himself at her, she deftly stepped aside and, as he passed her she drove the knife into his buttock, thus driving him through the flames. Smoke and flames belched from his breeches and with a shriek he threw himself upon the ground, rolling about and slapping at his crotch that was rapidly engulfed by the flames. Purity snatched up a pitcher of water that was standing next to the fire and threw it over his burning breeches.

"Let's hope that this has been a lesson to you. And, let's hope that the flames have quenched the thirst of that which hangs between your legs."

She walked to the fire and, removing the hare from the flames, she tore it in half and presented a portion to the rustic. "Take this and be on your way, scoundrel. And, I'll make you a promise that if our paths should cross again much worse will befall you."

The man jumped to his feet and, snatching the meat on offer, he stumbled away into the darkness. Purity listened with some amusement to his retreating footsteps.

In a way she was rather pleased with her experience. There was a lesson in it for her. If she was going to make fires in this open land, she had to be on her guard. Also, it was the first opportunity she had of putting her knowledge of self-defence into practice and she felt rather pleased with the results.

After she had eaten, she doused the fire and, rolling herself in a rug, she went to sleep.

Isn't the nasty man going to come back and cause more trouble for her?

No, my angel.

Will we meet him again?

Oh, yes.

When?

Very soon, I think. Inadvertently he is going to cause a lot of trouble.

Go on, then! I can't wait!

※

It was late morning in the market square. Although trade was brisk, it was immediately evident that something was wrong. The atmosphere was slightly tainted, providing a somewhat colourless feel to proceedings. This feeling of heaviness was not new. It had gradually beset the market and could be counted back to the time of the death of the king. The change in the market and its proceedings could be seen on two counts: firstly, the articles on sale were of inferior quality. Whereas the plaques, statues and other silver ware were once large and ornate, they were now much smaller and more drab in appearance. Even their former lustre now appeared to be dimmed.

Secondly, the lustre also had left the visages of the people. The light-hearted banter and smiles had gone. Whereas formerly potential buyers were enticed by friendly persuasion, methods had now changed and overall there was an air of frantic cajoling.

All this was a direct result of the queen's rule. She was in the process of plundering the best products from the silver mines. Fewer merchants were now visiting the city, since they had no need for inferior wares. And, above all this, taxes were raised. All this was gradually resulting in a shortage of food.

The drabness of the market place was also infiltrating the city. The once brightly painted houses and well-maintained statues were now becoming dowdy and the gardens and parks had an unkempt look about them. Vagrants and tramps were evermore in evidence and the sight of their starved corpses amongst the shrubs in the parks were increasingly common.

On this particular morning there was a man in the market, a traveller, who was trading his wares of fruit, vegetables and wheat. He soon realised that his supplies were in great demand and, as is usual with the unscrupulous, he soon raised his prices to double their worth. It was not long before he had sold all his wares and he made his way to a nearby tavern, his pockets filled with his ill-gotten gains. Here he sated himself with a bowl of mutton stew, after which he purchased a flagon of wine with which he intended to drink himself into a state of blissful oblivion. Nearby him a group of young men were in conversation. They were discussing their travels in distant lands and the miraculous sights they had encountered. As the wine flowed, their talk became more robust and their supposed adventures more wondrous. There were tales of the slaying of savage beasts, of single-handed combats against groups of bandits and of daring escapes from secure prisons and certain death. To all this our trader listened too with an avid ear, for he was keen to find an opening so that he may impose himself on the conversation. The chance presented itself when a young man recounted a particularly unlikely event that had befallen him.

"I remember once being captured by a band of marauding women, all of them beauties! For three weeks they held me captive and wined and dined me on only the best. All I wanted was supplied in abundance. All that was required of me was that I should mate with one of their group every night." His companions laughed uproariously. "In spite of all the food provided, I became as thin as a rake with all the effort and energy that was required from me. Eventually, my body became so emaciated and lean that I was able to make my escape through a grating in the cell in which I was held." More uproarious laughter.

It was now that our trader interposed himself:

"Gentlemen! Pardon me for intrudin', but I was listenin' with great interest to your tales of adventure. I also have a tale to tell which I believe you may find entertainin'."

"Speak up then, you rascal!" Cries one of the youths. "And, your tale better be good or we shall have the hide off you!"

"Well, a most terrible fate befell me whilst I was journeyin' towards your beautiful city. I was encamped in a clearin' by the side of the road and I had just prepared my evenin' meal when a woman walks into the light of the fire. She was most beautiful. I was very surprised by what I seen, since it is not often that one should see a woman travellin' on her ownsome. My immediate thought was that she was lost and, gallant person that I am, I jumped to my feet and enquired of her whether she needed any assistance. I was, however, utterly surprised to see her drawin' a long sword from the sheath by her side. She was also carryin' a bow and some arrows, a spear and a dagger in a scabbard on her leg. All these weapons she laid upon the ground within easy reach. She then, on pains of death, demanded that I should give her the hare, which was roastin', on the fire and she immediately consumed this. After she had eaten her fill of my catch, she insisted that I should remove my breeches. She claimed that she had not had the pleasure of a man's flesh for months, nay indeed, years, and she intended to have her fill of me. I naturally refused and with this she flew into a most terrible rage. She snatched up her dagger and drove it up to the hilt into my arm! Right here! See! You can see the scar she left! I had jumped to my feet in an effort to defend myself, but, quick as a flash, she snatched a firebrand with which she attacked me and set my breeches on fire! With some difficulty I managed to retrieve my own sword and, not bein' an unaccomplished swordsman myself, I managed to drive her off."

Uproarious laughter from the crowd: "You lying scoundrel! But, it is indeed a good tale and therefore we will pardon you your lies! Now, tell us! What did this vengeful beauty look like?"

With this our man told the only truth of his story and he proceeded to give a detailed description of the princess, Purity.

Now, it so happened that a small man with weasel features was sitting nearby, listening to all this frivolous conversation. On hearing the description of the princess, he finished his wine and, with a thoughtful look, he left the tavern.

The queen was in her chambers when the guards brought the weasel into her presence. She was with one of her councillors and they were busy compiling a new proclamation. It was her intention to impose an evening curfew

"Now then, Weasel. Why are you interrupting me?"

"I beg your majesty's pardon. But, I come from the tavern in the market square where I heard some news that may be of interest to your highness."

"You know, Weasel, you are really quite an ugly, treacherous little man."

"Thank you, your majesty."

"I really despise deceitful little men like you. Sometimes I have an overpowering desire to have you flogged, just for what you are. But, I suppose that, if a builder wishes to construct a good house, he sometimes has to resort to the use of pig's dung in the mortar. So, tell me! Swift, man! Before I submit to my urges!"

The weasel then related what he had heard and, on hearing his tale, the queen flew into a great rage. "So, the hunter has betrayed me! If there is treachery that I despise above all, then it is treachery against my own person! I pledge that the hunter will most sincerely regret his actions!"

And, saying so, she dismissed the two men in her company so that she could turn her thoughts to a course of action.

Ah! Poor hunter! I suppose he is going to get it in the neck? Mind you, I don't know why I call him the poor hunter. His behaviour up till now has not exactly been exemplary. Is she going to execute him?

She is going to have a good go, my angel. But, I would think that the hunter, with all his skills, might be a formidable enemy.

Shall we carry on?

Most certainly, my darling.

※

That night, as the hunter was sitting in front of his hearth, a knock came upon his door and, on opening it, he saw a young man standing there.

"The queen requests an audience, Hunter."

"What does she wish from me?"

"She told me to inform you that she has some further task for you for which you shall be well reimbursed."

So, the hunter put on his cloak and accompanied the young man to the palace. Since he expected no trouble, he left his sword behind. Even if he should have deigned to take his sword, he was well searched by the guards on entering the palace to ensure that he carried no arms. When he was shown into the queen's presence, she said to him:

"Hunter I was so impressed by the way in which you disposed of the princess. Will you relate the tale to me again so that I may wonder at your artfulness? But, this time, Hunter, (since we are partners in crime), I also want you to tell me how you really slayed the princess."

"Well, your majesty," replied the hunter. "For the benefit of the people, I had to tell of how she was attacked and killed by a silver tiger.

But, in truth, I shot her through the heart with my bow and arrows and buried her body deep in the forest where she would not be found."

"Is that so, Hunter?" Asked the queen. "I have just recent news that the princess has been seen, hale and bright and terrorising unsuspecting travellers." Saying this her face became contorted with anger. "You have betrayed my trust, Hunter! There is an ancient saying, Hunter: 'He who deals in treachery, shall flounder by his own device'. Now, what have you to say?"

Since his return the hunter's equanimity had been disturbed. Before he had met the princess, his goals in life had been simple and straight forward: he avoided human contact as far as possible; he asked for no favours from others and he offered none. But, perversely, in spite of the simple codes by which he lived, he was drawn by the lustre of gold and silver and he was therefore quite prepared to sell his favours. All this had now inexplicably changed. Since his return from the hunting trip, his days and his nights had been severely troubled. Against his wishes and much to his annoyance he had found himself bonded to Purity. She was constantly in his thoughts and he made a promise to himself that he would search her out, where ever she was, at the earliest opportunity. But, what concerned him most were the feelings of guilt that had beset him. Concern for others and guilt over his actions were totally alien to him. And now, with the queen's words, it was as if a sluice had been opened in his mind. All the guilt and anxiety poured out of his mind and he felt the pressure lifting from him. With a great feeling of relief he suddenly realised right from wrong, good from evil and he saw the course that he should take, what ever the consequences might be to himself. The hunter, realising that his actions had been uncovered, decided no longer to shield himself behind cautious words: "There is another ancient saying, your majesty: 'He who fraternises with dogs, shall suffer the fate of dogs'. I have travelled extensively with the lady, Purity, and I have learnt why she is beloved by all her people. I have also had the misfortune of gaining some knowledge of you and there is a fact that you may as well accept: for as long as your presence remains in this city, the people will hate and despise you. The only way that you will subject them is through fear."

The queen rose in anger and summoned her guards. The hunter, jumping to his feet, reached for his sword out of habit, but it was not there. The guards soon overpowered him and tied his hands and feet with twine.

"Take him to the dungeon and keep him safe for the night. Tomorrow he will be tried and executed. He shall be taken to the clearing outside the city wall where he will be tied to the tree of execution! You have spent your life hunting animals, now let them have a chance to feast on you! I would call that natural justice, don't you think so, Hunter? Now, remove him from my sight! And, mind you guard him well!"

I know the hunter did some evil things, but do you really think we should just let him die like this?

I don't know, my angel. What do you think?

I think we should maybe give him a chance to redeem himself. And, anyway, how is the queen going to prevent the people from finding out that Purity is still alive?

Well thought, my precious! Let us bend our minds to that!

Before we do that: can we have another look at the hunter's character? I mean, one minute he was a solitary, austere, rather frightening and unscrupulous character. But, now, suddenly he has become a champion of the princess. Is this likely?

Yes, I think so. I knew someone like that. Shall I tell you about her?

Yes, please.

She was one of my teachers at school. At the school I went to teachers often doubled up on subjects. For instance, our geography teacher was also our language teacher and the sports master doubled up as history teacher. (He was particularly useless at both.) At the start of one term the lady in question joined the school as science teacher. She was a tall, gangly, sexless unattractive woman who inspired charmless fear in all the students. I was particularly bad at chemistry. I just could not grasp all those chemical symbols. But, with the advent of this lady and the fear she instilled in me, I learnt everything like a parrot and passed my tests. (No need to say that I forgot all I learned as soon as I took my exams)

Now, at that time the librarian at our school was a doddery old boy who was about to retire. When he left at the end of term, our lady doubled up as science teacher and librarian. I was very keen on reading and I frequented the library often. To my surprise she noted my interest in books and she started recommending reading material. Soon after that we became friends. We would frequently find ourselves in animated discussions on books and authors and I lost all my fear of her. Underneath this charmless plain exterior there lived a beautiful, romantic and very sexy woman. I believe that she hated science as much as I did and that her real love was the romance and thrill of literature. When I eventually left school, she was the only teacher I missed.

So, you see, my darling, I would hope that the hunter was the same. He always had good in him. Circumstances just never allowed him to express himself.

She sighs: Thank you for telling me about your friend. I will view the hunter in a different light from now on. Tell me what happened to him.

Now, at all cost, the queen had to prevent rumours concerning the survival of Purity from spreading amongst the people of the city. Like all tyrants she had a natural tendency towards paranoia and she believed that the people would be spurred to insurrection if they should come to believe that the princess was still alive. She therefore devised some strategies to quash all unnecessary rumours.

First of all the scoundrel who told about his confrontation in the wilderness was sought out. By a combination of some threats and a substantial some of money he was persuaded to leave the city in haste. Secondly, the four youths to whom he had told his story were found and dealt with. They were lured to a deserted area of the park where they were attacked and murdered. A rumour was then circulated that they had all killed each other in a drunken brawl. All that was left now was to deal with the hunter.

That night the hunter was imprisoned in a damp and dismal little cell in the dungeons. The cell contained no creature comforts, such as padded furniture or rugs for warmth. His over mantle and his sandals were removed and he was shackled and chained to one of the walls of the cell. Soon he also realised that he was not to be given any sustenance.

This then were the circumstances in which the hunter was left, (in which he believed to be), his final night. Since he was unable to sleep, he used the time left to him to contemplate his recent deeds and, somewhat to his surprise, he discovered within himself a change of attitude. He found that he did not regret his words and demeanour towards the dark queen. His mind and soul was also once again filled with that feeling of peace and cleansing that he experienced earlier that evening when he confronted the queen. It was as if his whole being had been infused with a new and pure consciousness. This, however did not mean that he was prepared to accept death without a struggle and for the rest of the night he strained with all his thoughts to discover a means of escape. Needless to say, none came to him and as the light of dawn filtered through the small window in the cell, he finally accepted his fate.

On the morning a trial was hastily arranged. He would be tried in the market square at noon and all the city folk were invited to attend. In spite of the queen's efforts to suppress any rumours concerning the hunter and the princess, strange news soon spread throughout the city. It was said that the princess was still alive and that the hunter attacked the queen and her guards single-handedly, but that he was overpowered and condemned to death. With this news the hunter gained sympathy from the folk with the consequences that few of them made the effort to attend the hearing.

As the time bell signalled noon the hunter was led onto a stage in the market square. He was bound, gagged and hooded and after all had assembled, the charges against him were read. These were as follows:

"You are charged with taking a member of the royal family on a hunting expedition into the wilderness, an area that is eminently unsuitable for a lady. Here you were negligent in your duties in so far as providing adequate protection for her royal highness. We are also informed by reliable witnesses that you did not only neglect her, but that you also ultimately ravaged and murdered the princess and that you buried her body deep in the forest where she would not be found." (Suffice it to say that none of these "reliable witnesses" were actually produced)

After the charges had been read, there was a short conference amongst the queen's councillors and a verdict of guilty was pronounced. Then his sentence was read. The hunter was to be taken to a clearing outside the city walls where he would be tied to the tree of execution. Here he would be left until such time as he starved to death or was devoured by the wild animals that roamed the land outside the city.

He was then led away and the crowd dispersed in uneasy silence. It is in the nature of tyrants that they are never overly subtle in dealing with their subjects and this was amply demonstrated in the trial of the hunter. Although he had no great friends among the people, it was obvious to all who attended that this was a mistrial. Its main effect was to antagonise the people even more towards the queen and her new council.

The hunter was once more confined to the dungeon from where he would be taken in the early evening to the place of execution.

Oh dear! When are we going to save him?

I think we should do it sooner rather than later, my darling, otherwise his goose will be well and truly cooked. But, before we do that, I also believe that we should take another look at what is happening to Purity.

After a few days travel, Purity had traversed the open country between the forest and the mountain range she was heading for. Throughout she behaved with caution and discretion and, although she encountered many fellow travellers, her journey was remarkably uneventful. After her encounter with the felon who wished to ravage her, she had cautioned herself to become most watchful and this she did with good effect.

As she drew nearer to what she believed to be a mountain range, she realised that what lay ahead of her was instead a series of steep hills. This lifted her spirits, because she believed that she was imminently capable of crossing these. As she reached the foot of the hills in the early evening, she decided to rest here for the night in preparation of the next stage of her journey.

As she sat by her campfire that night, she fell to thinking and her mind dwelt on the events, not only of the last days and weeks, but also of the years past. She thought of the happy times she had spent in the palace, of her tutors, of her hunting dogs and, especially of her father. She was filled with such a longing that she believed her heart would burst. For the first time since she had left with the hunter she felt absolutely vulnerable and hot tears stung her eyes and fell down her cheeks. After she had been sitting thus and crying for some long time, she eventually gained control of her emotions and she rolled herself in a rug and prepared for sleep.

Sleep, however, did not come for a long time and when she eventually drifted into slumber, her sleep was fitful and restless and she was troubled by strange dreams. She was riding in the forest with the hunter by her side, but instead of talking to her about his trade, he was telling her in a hoarse and cracked voice that the dark queen had discovered that she was still alive and that she was on their trail. When she looked up she saw that the hunter was wearing no cloak and that his feet were bare. His hands were shackled in front of him and he had great difficulty in holding the reins of the horse. Heavy chains also hung from his legs and these were jingling loudly as they snagged on passing branches. She glanced over her shoulder and behind her the forest parted and she saw with fear and alarm the queen and some soldiers bearing down on them. The hunter was urging her to ride faster, but in front of her stretched an impenetrable wall of high thorn brush. Behind her she could hear the rattling of the hunter's chains and the shouts of the soldiers and from all sides the trees were reaching out with branches as of gnarled fingers with which they clutched at her hair and clothing. Suddenly she felt long fingers entangling themselves in her hair. She did not know whether it was man or tree, but she was violently pulled from her horse and she was falling backward into space. She was plunging into a deep chasm. Above her she saw the blue of the sky diminishing until the top of the chasm suddenly snapped shut and she was surrounded by a dense darkness. She knew that she was falling into the underworld. Far below her she could hear a tumult of voices, shouting, screeching and sobbing and suddenly she was in their midst. As she hit the ground, she awoke.

She sat up and rubbed her eyes. Her face was drenched in sweat. She looked up at the stars and realised that dawn was still a long way off. What an awful dream! Something beyond its macabre aspect disturbed her. Intuitively she knew that the hunter was in trouble, but she was depressingly aware that there was nothing she could do to help him. Thinking about the dream, she realised that she was trapped between the past and the future: A past that was closed to her and to which she could not return and, in front of her, a future that was obscured by the unknowable.

It took a long time for her to drift back into sleep, but when she did her nightmarish dreams were replaced with a vision of her father. They were sitting side by side in one of the rooms of the palace. They were not talking. He was reading from a scroll. She was looking at him and he was radiating an aura of peace and tranquillity. Without words he soothed her mind and when she once again awoke she felt calmed and reassured. She rose with the dawn and prepared herself for the next stage of her journey, the nightmare of the night being consigned to her subconscious as a dim and distant echo.

After she had broken her fast, she packed her belongings and went on her way.

At first she made (what she believed to be), steady and easy progress. The lower slopes were gentle with many paths leading upwards and onwards. However, she soon realised that most of these tracks ended abruptly and without warning. Consequently, she was forced on countless occasions to retrace her steps. So, by late morning she had only made little progress. She was a steadfast and resourceful young lady and she did not allow her spirits to falter.

After much to-ing and fro-ing, she eventually stumbled upon a narrow track that appeared to lead directly towards a steep hill in the distance. With trepidation she followed this road. She did not hold out much hope. She believed that this track would fade and falter as did all the others she had so far encountered. It was therefore with great relief and considerable surprise that she found herself standing at the foot of the great hill by mid-afternoon.

Since the light was still good, she decided to continue on her journey. She started to climb and she soon found that the track was gently spiralling up and around the hill, a fact that made her crossing much easier than she had feared.

It was in the early evening that her progress was unexpectedly and cruelly halted. As she rounded a small outcrop of rocks, she looked down and stopped in her tracks with a cry of anxiety and surprise. At her feet lay a ravine, not very wide, but very deep. The track had come to an abrupt end. She felt thoroughly downcast. How was she ever going to cross this obstacle? Was all her days journey in vain? Would she be forced to retrace her steps all the way to the beginning and start again?

She decided to explore the top of the ravine and to this purpose she moved to her left, but very soon her way was obstructed by a dense copse of thorn bushes. On moving to her right she found the same. In the distance in front of her she could hear the sound of what she believed to be a waterfall. However, there was no way of confirming this, since her view was totally obscured by the bushes.

The light was now fading and night was fast approaching. This fact at least prohibited any further decisions and actions on her part for the present. She had no choice but to stay here for the night and to review her situation in the light of day.

She found some shelter under an overhang of the outcrops of rocks where she stowed her meagre possessions. She wrapped herself in a rug and, with a stone to pillow her head, she soon drifted into the deep, dreamless sleep of the just and weary.

As it is with those who have been trained to survive by their wits, she woke suddenly with a clear and wakeful mind. Above her the stars were shining in a clear, cloudless sky, but she hardly noticed them. She knew that something was afoot, but she was uncertain of the cause for her unease. Then she heard it: a faint scratching noise and a mewling as of a kitten. She threw off the rug with which she was covered and quietly rose to her feet. From her store of armoury she selected a particularly fearsome dagger. This was not just an ordinary dagger. It consisted of a central handle grip with a thin, sharp blade at one end and a particularly evil looking spike at the other.

Leaving the shelter of the rocks, she surveyed her surroundings and strained to hear from which direction the disturbance came. She moved to the edge of the ravine and looked down. Far below she espied something brightly gleaming. She soon realised that it was a river, and that the gleam was the reflection of the moon on the smooth surface of the water.

There it was again! That noise! A sound of scratching and a whimper. It was emanating from the other side of the rocky outcrop where she had been reposing.

Clutching her knife she moved around the rocks. At first she could see nothing untoward. A very large stone had become dislodged from the top of the pile of rocks. It had fallen in front of a shallow cave, partially obstructing the entrance. The beams of the moon were shining directly into the cave and reflected in its light against the back wall was crouched the small figure of the young of a silver tiger.

Immediately she realised what must have happened. Very likely the mother had left her kitten to go hunting for food and while she was away the rock had come tumbling down, thus trapping the young tiger.

The little creature was too small to climb across the rock. At intervals it would dart forward and scrabble frantically at the obstruction.

With the realisation of what had happened, her blood ran cold. Where was the mother right now? Although she had never seen a live silver tiger, she had heard many tales of their ferocity. It was said that no man would ever confront one of these creatures by himself. She had to get away from this place as soon as possible. But, as she turned to leave, it dawned on her that the mother would be unable to rescue her young. The gap between the top of the fallen rock and the roof of the cave was too narrow. She had no choice in the matter; she had to help the little creature to escape. Until the morning she was effectively trapped on the edge of the ravine and she could not afford to have a dangerous beast prowling about.

In order to free both hands, she planted the dagger into the earth, blade upward. The stone was extremely heavy, but she was a fit and strong young girl and gradually, inch-by-inch she moved the rock outwards until she had enough room to put both hands into the cave and lift the young tiger to safety. It was no more than a few weeks old and as tame as a house kitten. She took it in her arms and rose to her feet. As she turned round, the mother launched herself. In a streak of silver she flew at the girl, claws extended and slashing down towards her exposed face.

And, I think we should leave it there for the time being, my angel.

No! You can't do that! That is unfair.

Don't worry, my darling. I would just like to give my voice a rest and I would also like to collect my thoughts.

Shall we stay with Purity for a while?

No. We will let her fight with the tiger for a little. We are returning for the present to the city. I believe the oracle may have something up his sleeve. Let's see what the old rascal has in mind. By the way, how do you feel? Are you tired?

Oh, no! I am definitely not tired! We must go on as soon as you had a little rest.

The oracle is sitting beside a table in a small room off the inner court of the temple. He is writing on a parchment. There is movement at the door. He glances up. The high priest enters.

"I greet you, Oracle."

He rises: "I greet you, Holy Father."

"Have you heard the news, Oracle?""

"I have heard much news, High Priest; most of it bad and, more than likely, most of it false. Have you noticed, Holy One, how bad news spreads at the speed of a fire burning in a wheat field on a windy day?

"I have indeed, Oracle. Good news also has a habit of slumbering until the evening sun has set. Then it will rise slowly and make itself known to those whom it encounters on its leisurely way. On the other hand, bad news will rise with the dawn and rampage through the land and roar its message to all and sundry. At present it is rather difficult to estimate the worth of the rumours which are flying about, but we may as well sit for a while and share and deliberate."

They sit: "Now, tell me, High Priest. What have you heard?"

"I have heard that the hunter had been condemned to death. The charges against him were that he had been negligent in his care of the princess, Purity, and that he had finally ravaged and murdered her. It has to be acknowledged that the hunter does not have many friends amongst the people of the city, but amongst all those who attended the trial, there is a feeling that the charges against him were manufactured."

"I have heard the same, Holy Father, but this is indeed not the worse news that has come to my ears."

Tell me, Oracle. What have you heard?"

"As you well know, Holy One, I have ears and eyes all over the city. How else would I be aware of what my people feel and think? Well, I am informed that a traveller was in a tavern yesterday and that he told tales of an encounter with a female personage in the wilderness. Most of what he told were deemed to be fables, but his description of the young lady was most surely that of our princess."

"This is indeed incredible news, Oracle! On the one hand this is the most joyous news I have heard for a long time, for our princess is alive! On the other hand it makes my blood run with a chill to think that there is so much evil about that would allow our princess to be wandering unprotected in the wilderness."

"Oh, High Priest! It is not only our princess who is stranded in the wilderness. I am afraid that our city has also entered into a wild place and it will take much effort to restore both to their rightful place in the light."

"What do you suggest we do now, Oracle?"

"I have given it much thought, Holy One, and I have come to the following conclusions: it appears to me that the hunter was under instructions from the queen to get rid of the princess, most likely by killing her. He must have had second thoughts and let her escape. And, now she has discovered that the hunter had lied to her on his return and she has decided to revenge herself on him. Obviously, she cannot let it be known why she is punishing the hunter, therefore the false charges. So, I believe that we have little choice in the matter: the hunter has to be saved. He is the only one who can find and protect her."

"And, how shall we achieve this?"

"I have already set plans in motion, Holy One."

The high priest smiles: Oh, Oracle. If the people only knew the extent of the duties you take upon yourself."

"It is best that they don't, Holy Father. As long as they believe that I am a frail old man who only deals with spiritual matters, they will tell me all their little secrets. If they should discover that I also sometimes involve myself in earthly, practical matters, they will bring forth as little as a closed, empty sarcophagus."

"I suppose you are right. Well, I will leave you to your scheming." He rises and leaves the room.

In the early evening a vagrant can be seen to enter the park. He strolls at a leisurely pace amongst the flowerbeds and lawns. On occasions he would confront a passer-by and extend his begging bowl. Mostly he is either ignored or chased away. He eventually sees a young man sitting on a bench. He is reading from a scroll. Slowly the beggar approaches and stops in front of the young man. They have a brief conversation. The beggar extends his bowl and the man takes a coin from his cloak and drops it into the bowl. The beggar moves away.

After some time the young man rolls up his scroll and rises from the bench. He leaves the park and makes his way to the foreign quarters. It is here where those are housed who are not citizens of the city. He is of a slender built and his step is light and graceful, but on closer inspection it can be noticed that he is possessed of a wiry strength. His complexion is fair and his hair and beard are long and golden.

On reaching a certain house, he knocks twice and enters. He finds himself in a room with three others. From their complexion and build it is immediately obvious that they are all from the same land. After some conversation the man from the park takes his leave. Sometime later his three companions follow, each leaving on his own and with a short interval between each. They melt into the crowd and make their way to the temple.

✵

The oracle rises as the four young men enter the room. He speaks: "I am what was; I am the here and now; I am the future; I am the truth; I am the mirror of my people; I am the Oracle; I greet you."

They all bow and the lanky young man from the park steps forward and speaks. It is evident that he acts as leader and spokesman: "We greet you, Oracle and we are indeed honoured to be in your presence. But, if truth be told, we are at a loss to know why we should be here."

"Pray, be seated and I will make all clear. Now, as you can tell from my greeting, there is not much in this city that escapes my notice. I know that the four of you hail from the land of the Canyon-Dwellers.

You have been living in our city for four years, intent on your studies." He points to each man as he continues: "You are training to be a surgeon; and, you are a member of the brotherhood of master builders and making a study of our architecture; you are here to learn all about mining engineering; and, you have been joining our astrologers to learn what you can from the stars. I also know that your king was a true friend and ally to our deceased ruler. Now, tell me: what is your impression of the current state of this city? Have no fear. You may speak freely and honestly."

The surgeon speaks: "We are deeply concerned for the welfare of this glorious city. Our loyalty was towards the king and the princess, but they are now both gone. The city has now changed. The people go about their business in fear and anguish. We do not believe that those who rule at present act in the interest of the people. Indeed, it is in our minds to go back to our own land as soon as possible."

"No doubt you are aware of what befell the princess?"

"Indeed we are. She died whilst on a hunting trip."

"Then, what would you say if I told you that the princess is still alive?"

"We would indeed jump for joy! But, this cannot be! The hunter was tried for her death and found guilty! If she is alive, why is she not here to rally her people?"

"It is my belief that the queen orchestrated her death and that she used the hunter to this purpose. It appears that the hunter had second thoughts and released her into the wilderness. I also believe that he informed her of the queen's intent and that he urged her not to return to the city. I need some one to find her and rescue her from the wilderness."

The young surgeon looks at his compatriots: "What do you say, fellows? Shall we help to find the princess?"

The master builder shrugs and answers with gruff indifference: "Why not? As you stated, it was in our minds to return to the canyon and it is on our way."

The surgeon looks at the remaining two. Their features indicate that they are brothers. Their demeanour is languid, what in modern terms may be called, "laid back". "What about you two? Are you up for it?"

The astrologer smiles lazily and speaks: "Yes, why not? The stars in the wilderness are the same as here in the city. I may even get a better view of them there."

The philosopher yawns: "I agree. My head is rather full of unanswered questions. A gentle stroll through the countryside may help to clear my mind."

The oracle sighs with relief: "I thank you, my friends. But, before you go on your way, there is another favour I beg of you. We have to save the hunter. He knows the country as well as you do and his help will be invaluable to you."

"This may be difficult. He will be well guarded."

"I have learnt that four of the queen's men have been delegated to guard the hunter. But, not many of the city folk will go to witness the execution. I know my people. Although none of them befriended the hunter, it is in their nature to deplore any injustice."

The surgeon rises: "Well, the hour is getting late and we have much to do. Let's be on our way and see what can be done."

"I wish you farewell and may the gods go with you. And, if they should not, do not fear, because I will also keep an eye on you."

They all rise and leave the room.

They will have to be quick if they are going to save the hunter. Will they succeed?

We'll have to wait and see, my angel. But, I think it is time we returned to Purity. Remember, we left her in rather a precarious situation. The last we saw of her a big old cat was trying to kill her.

※

As Purity rose and turned, she saw the silver tiger streaking towards her, claws extended and slashing down at her face. All that followed, happened in the wink of an eye. As she rose to her feet, she stepped on a small, loose stone and this saved her life. The stone slipped from under her foot and she fell sideways. The tiger arrowed across her and the weight of its body drove her to the ground. As she hit the earth, the air was driven from her lungs, her head struck the ground with a thud and all went dark.

After a short while, she regained her senses. Her body felt bruised and battered. A heavy weight was on her legs, pinning her to the ground. She looked down and saw the tiger stretched across the lower part of her body. Why was it so still? Why was it not attacking and savaging her?

With some effort she withdrew her legs from under the tiger and rose to her knees. At first she could see nothing to explain its lack of motion. Slowly and cautiously she moved closer to the beast and then she gasped with surprise. In missing its aim the tiger had plunged to the earth. It had fallen upon the dagger that she had planted near the rocks. The sharp blade had pierced its throat and the point of the blade was protruding from the back of its neck. It was dead.

She looked at the sleek body, the long, silver hair and the extended claws and she shuddered. She was filled with a mixture of relief and sorrow; sorrow for the passing of this beautiful creature and relief that she had survived the fearsome attack. The gods had indeed been with her. It was she who should be dead now.

She heard a soft mewling and looked down. The little cub was nuzzling its mother. She noticed that the mother's teats were full with milk. She picked up the little tiger and presented it to a teat. "Drink up, Little One. This will be the last feed you get from this source. Then, what is to be done with you?"

While the little tiger was feeding, she walked back to the ravine. It was beginning to get light. The sun was just poking its head over the furthest hills. After a short while it was light enough for her to survey her surroundings. How was she going to cross this ravine? She sat down and contemplated the opposite bank.

Then she looked down and her heart leapt. In the dusk of the previous evening she did not notice the small steps that led down to a ledge on the right. These steps were hardly wide enough for one person to negotiate. Should she go and explore before she moved on? She decided not to. If the steps were there, it meant that others had gone that way and therefore she would take a chance and follow.

She collected and arranged her belongings and then she went back to the dead tiger. The little cub was crouching forlornly nearby. "You will have to come with me, my little friend. I could not leave you here to die. How I will provide for you, I do not know. But, no doubt the gods will show the way."

She made a carrying sling of her cloak, which she tied around her neck. She placed the little tiger in the sling, took her belongings on her back and descended the steps.

The steps led down to a narrow ledge that skirted the wall, some forty feet above the floor of the ravine. Her view ahead was obstructed, for some way ahead, the ravine bore to the right. Hugging the wall closely, she moved along with care. On reaching the bend she noticed with relief that the ledge was getting wider, but turning the corner she stopped in despair at what she saw in front of her. A great rush of water was cascading over the rim of the wall, crashing into the river below. There appeared to be no way of passing this obstacle.

Then she noted something that stirred her curiosity. Near the wall, instead of an impenetrable curtain of water, there appeared to be a dense vapour obscuring her view. On moving closer she saw with surprise that there was indeed a passage underneath the waterfall. The current was gushing with such force that it was missing the ledge below. With some trepidation she entered this watery tunnel.

The tunnel was not very long, but she discovered that the rush of water above was drawing all the air from her lungs. Panting and fighting for breath, she moved along the ledge. She had to be very careful. The ground below her feet was slippery and the light was not very good. About half way along the tunnel, she looked up to see what was ahead and this was nearly her undoing. The water caught the top of her head and threw her sideways. Her feet slipped from under her and she fell, sliding towards the edge of the ledge. Frantically she clutched at the ground below her and, as she was about to plunge over the edge, she found some purchase on a small bulge of rock. With great effort she scrambled back to the wall of the ravine. Gingerly she rose to her feet and, taking extra care, she traversed the last few yards and exited from the tunnel.

With relief she stepped out into the warm morning sunshine and she sat down to rest and collect herself. She felt bruised and battered, but she was alive and for this she was grateful.

She looked ahead and saw with joy that a series of steps led down to the floor of the ravine and onto the riverbank. Although the river was flowing swiftly, it was but shallow at this point and a row of stepping stones were so arranged as to help the traveller across. From the opposite bank a set of steps led to the top of the ravine. After a short rest she traversed the ravine. She was across! Ahead of her, leading into the distance, stretched a wide, beckoning track.

Wow! Our girl is lucky to be alive!

You are right, my angel. After the events of the previous night I think we can safely assume that she is blessed with a fair amount of luck and she is riding it. She is obviously a survivor and it bodes well for her future.

Are we following her progress, or are we returning to the hunter?

I think we should go back and see how the hunter is doing. We will leave Purity to have a well-deserved rest.

At dusk the hunter was taken from the dungeon to the tree of execution. As tradition dictated, he was dressed in a white robe and mounted on top of an open white carriage, drawn by six pure white horses. The carriage was escorted by the queen's guard, all dressed in their ceremonial uniform. At the front of the procession rode a lone horseman on a black horse, he also being dressed from head to foot in black. As the procession passed, he would ring a bell and call out the charges against the prisoner to the crowd as well as the proclamation of death.

The procession left the city by the southern portals and made its way to a tall tree in a clearing some four hundred paces from the city walls. Here the hunter was dismounted, stripped of all clothing and seated against the tree. His arms were raised above his head and firmly secured with ropes to the tree. All then left, except for four guards who retreated to a small watchtower on the edge of the clearing. The tower was far enough from the tree to allow a clear view of the hunter whilst not disturbing any visiting animals.

And so, the hunter sat in silence and discomfort: the bare skin of his back was painfully rubbing against the rough bark of the tree and his wrists were being chafed raw by the ropes that tied him. The insects of the early evening were paying their customary visit and he was plagued by swarms of moths that fluttered around his head and face and gnats and mosquitoes were feeding voraciously on his tender parts. He was utterly exhausted due to the fact that he had no sleep the previous night. He knew that there was no escaping death and he had resigned himself to his fate. He therefore tried to close himself to his troubles and, as nature demands it, his tired mind eventually came to his aid. After some time he drifted into a fitful doze.

The intended curfew was not to be imposed until the following night, thus allowing the city folk the opportunity to come and inspect the demise of the prisoner. However, as the oracle rightly suspected, not many had the stomach for this. Only a few came and they also left after a short while, leaving the clearing, the tree and the watchtower in silence.

Inside the tower the guards were taking their ease. They did not expect any trouble from the city folk. As queen's men they looked on the inhabitants with scorn and contempt. They were so easily subdued. Privately they all wished for some insurrection and some fighting. They were all bored with this inactivity, but somehow they did not expect these spineless folk to rise up and relieve their tedium.

Now, in the early gloom of the evening and by the light of a lantern, they were playing a game of dice on a wooden table that was set in the centre of the tower. Each man in turn would shake the dice in a small metal cup and cast them in the middle of the table. The numbers on the dice would be added together and, intermittently, coins would pass back and forth from the little piles of silver that was stacked in front of each man. But, even this game of chance did not fill them with enthusiasm. One of the guards spoke:

"Dog's breath! This is going to be a long night!"

"Don't fret," said another guard. "Some folk may come to cheer us all up. Or, even some animals to help themselves to the bastard by the tree."

"I don't believe the city folk will be seen here tonight" replied a third. "These folk have no stomach for a little blood sport. They will all be skulking in their holes by now. And, if no animals come to feed, we will have to sit here all night and cut his throat at dawn. I am of a mind to let him feel my knife right now. What I would not do for a bowl of broth and a mug of ale!"

"I know what you mean. I have to admit an evening in the Market Tavern would be preferable to this. And, after the broth and ale, I would not be averse to helping myself to a portion of the wench who serves there."

The fourth guard speaks: "Be quiet, you old goat. Pay attention to the game. You owe me six silver bits."

Then, from the direction of the city came the sound of voices, laughing and singing as they drew nearer. Out of the gloom, four young men appeared with packs on their backs and carrying walking staves.

"Who goes there!" called one of the guards.

"We are four travellers and we are returning to our home land!"

"Step into the light so that we may take a look at you." They moved closer. "Is it not rather late for travelling?"

"Oh, well. We felt rested and we decided to make the first stage of our journey at night while the air was cool. And, anyway, it provided us with an opportunity to stop and see the prisoner. How are things with him?"

"We do not expect any fun from the animals for some time yet and very few from the city had been here tonight. I am afraid the folk around here are far too soft for my liking. The sight of a little blood makes them cower like dogs."

"Well, we have come for some excitement. A good slaughter will give us plenty to talk about on our journey. May we join you in the tower so that we can have a good view of proceedings?"

"Certainly you may."

"But first," said one of the travellers, "let us have a look at the prisoner."

They surrounded the hunter and jeered and one of them prodded him in the ribs. The hunter, who was dozing fitfully, started awake and glared at the four young men.

"Wake up, you scoundrel!" shouted one of them. He reached forward and tweaked the hunter's nose. The guards laughed with great gusto. As the young man leant towards the hunter, he whispered: "Take courage. Stay alert and be ready to leave soon."

A look of surprise showed in the hunter's eyes and he nodded imperceptibly. Fortunately, since the guards were some distance away in the gloom, this exchange was lost to them.

The four young men entered the tower. After a short while one of them took a small cup and some dice from his bag and they began to play a game. The guards noticed that gold coins frequently changed hands.

"What are you playing?"

"It is a gambling game from our land. We often play it to pass the time." And, they explained the rules of the game to the guards.

"Since it is so quiet, may we join you?"

"Indeed you may!" And, they all sat down to play.

Then, another of the young men took a flask from his pack. "Would you join me in a drink?"

"Most kind of you, Young Sir. What have you there?"

"Some good wine."

The flask was passed from man to man. The guards did not notice that the four travellers only pretended to drink. It was not long before the guards became drowsy and soon fell into a deep sleep where they were sitting.

The astrologer addressed the surgeon: "You did not poison them, did you?"

"No. They are only in a deep sleep. The drug will wear off by the morning and we should be well on our way by then. With any luck it will be too late for them to pursue us successfully."

The master builder growled: "You may as well have poisoned the vermin. It is my bet that the queen will dispose of them anyway."

"Quick now. We must make haste."

Swiftly they entered the clearing, untied the hunter and dressed him in a riding cloak. He had many surprised questions to ask, but they urged him to be silent and to make haste. There would be sufficient time later to answer all his inquiries.

Leaving the clearing, they made there way to a small wood where five horses were tethered. Mounting the horses, they left the city at a gallop.

At dawn, the four guardsmen were found unconscious on the floor of the watchtower and the hunter gone. The guards were removed to the palace where all was tried to revive them without success. It was not until late the following morning that they were in a state of mind to be interrogated, but this will be the subject of another part of the tale.

Well, at least help is on the way for Purity now.

Don't be too hasty, my darling. It will take them a long time to find her and many things can still happen.

Shall we see how she is doing?

Yes. Let's.

After crossing the ravine, Purity found her travels to be less fraught with difficulty. It was as if the gods had tested her by placing obstacles in her way, but having passed their examination of her courage and resolve, they were now smiling on her. The road she was on was wide and well trodden and her descent of the great hill was gentle. She had other hills to cross, but the road skirted their lower slopes, thus avoiding any strenuous or hazardous climbing. After some days she exited from the range of hills and once again she found herself in a land of lush, grass-covered valleys. The land ahead of her was criss-crossed with a myriad of gently flowing streams and the scent of summer flowers hung heavy on the summer air.

She frequently met other travellers, but her disguise served her well. Her head was always well covered and she took care not to show too much of her face. She was also tall and she walked with an easy, graceful step. All who met her took her for a handsome youth.

There was, however, a small problem that occupied her mind: This involved the care of her unexpected passenger, the silver tiger cub. Until now her only experience of wild animals was in the hunting of them. Never had she been required to care for them. But, she was a resourceful young woman and she bent her mind to this task with accustomed vigour.

She had heard it said that the silver tiger was untameable, but she soon found, (much to her own surprise and delight), that the little cub responded well enough to her voice and touch. For a short while the cub, (as nature demanded), pined for its mother, but because it was so young, its memories of the wild were but fuzzy. At all times she gently tended to the cub and coaxed it to her mind and soon they became inseparable and the little creature snuggled close to her in the sling in which she carried it, nuzzling its head under her chin. She became fearful that it might be harmed by strangers and to this purpose she jealously hid its existence from them.

Feeding the little cub presented her with some problems at first. Whilst travelling through the hills she fed it on small pieces of well mashed, roasted meat and although the cub consumed these, its young digestion suffered sorely under such harsh treatment. But, as they left the hills and entered the grassy vales, she noted a number of well-scattered smallholdings where goats were kept. From the farmers she begged or stole some precious, nourishing goat's milk. The milk she mixed with the blood of young deer or hares and on this nutritious diet the cub soon rallied and grew strong.

She was now confronted with a new difficulty: the cub was becoming too big to carry with ease, but still too small to walk long distances. She had to find somewhere to shelter for a while. In such shelter the tiger could be allowed to grow strong. With this in mind, she scouted the land for a suitable place.

Surely, it should not be too difficult for her to find somewhere to rest, should it?

Ah, my darling! I think she had become rather cautious about where she stopped after her encounter with the brigand. You also have to bear it in mind that she would become more noticeable to passing strangers if she stayed in one place.

I see what you mean. Then, where would she stay?

Well, let's find out, shall we?

※

In the affair of finding a dwelling-place for herself and the tiger cub, it once again appeared as if fortune and the gods were smiling upon her. One day she left a valley and, passing over the crest of a hill, she saw, spread in front of her, a wide, open space. As far as the eye could see, the terrain appeared to be completely uninhabited. But, what drew her attention was a most peculiar feature, set well to the left and far from the road. Here, in isolation, stood a tall, slender hill, somewhat in the shape of a watchtower. She walked along until she was level with the hill and then she veered off the road and made her way towards it.

On reaching the hill she saw that it was indeed very steep, but she also noted that it was well covered in vegetation and footholds, thus providing an easy climb. She left her possessions and the cub at the foot of the hill and made her ascent. As she neared the peak, she found herself on a wide ledge that was carpeted in a soft spread of moss. From the back of the ledge rose a shear wall of rock that stretched to the top of the hill. She moved to the cliff face and brushed the vegetation aside, intent on climbing the rest of the way. Instead, she found herself in the entrance of a large cave. She stared in amazement and, entering the cave, she laughed with joy.

She found herself in a well-ventilated chamber. The roof of the cave was high enough for her to stand erect. The rays of the sun shone dimly through the plant curtain at the entrance, providing ample light within the chamber and the floor was covered in a dense carpet of green moss. It would make an ideal dwelling place. Here the tiger and she would be safe from danger of passers-by.

Then, something in the corner of the cave caught her eye. On the floor stood a square rock with a flat surface. On top of the rock were, what appeared to be the burnt remains of an animal. The rock and the remains had all the appearances of an altar. By the side of the altar stood an empty jar. On closer inspection she decided that it was many months since the apparent offering had been made. The ashes looked old and grey and the jar smelt musty with a faint odour of stale wine. The wine must have evaporated and for this to happen, many moons must have passed.

She looked down at the floor and here she found further evidence that this cave must have been used at some time in the past as a sacred place. Trapped within the moss-covered floor she espied some seeds of barley and wheat. She noted with interest that much of the seed had taken root within the moss and were beginning to sprout. This fact confirmed her suspicion that the cave had not been visited for a long time. But, who was to say that none would return? Would she be safe here? She pondered for a while and then, on reflection she decided to take a chance. She supposed that any unexpected visitors would approach the hill from the road and from the entrance of the cave she was provided with a fine view in that direction. She felt certain that she would not be surprised. She was also somewhat weary of this aimless wandering and she needed somewhere to rest for a while. She persuaded herself that she would not remain here for too long and her mind was set.

She stepped back onto the ledge and surveyed her surroundings. In front of her lay the road and she noted with satisfaction that she could see along its way for some considerable distance from her vantage point. On the other side of the road, a long way away, she thought that she could see a slight haze and she presumed that it was the smoke from a settlement, but since it was so far away, she felt no alarm. To left and right of her the plateau on which the hill stood stretched for some leagues. No discernable roads crossed this area. She noted that the ledge upon which she stood lead away from the cave to her left. Cautiously she made her way along the ledge until she reached the angle of the hill from where she could see the terrain behind her new dwelling-place. Once again she noted with satisfaction that the plateau stretched for many leagues with no visible roads upon it.

She returned to the entrance of the cave and swiftly she descended the hill and in stages she transported the cub and her possessions to the ledge and the cave. In the late afternoon she sat in front of her new dwelling and conversed with the little tiger:

"We will rest here for a while, little one. I did not realise until now just how tired I am of travelling. None will disturb us here. We shall be at peace. Here you will be allowed to grow and become strong. I do not know how long we will remain here, but that is of little importance. We will allow time to shape our future."

And so, the young princess and the tiger cub settled in their cave high on the hill. The months passed and summer faded into autumn. During this time the little creature grew from a cub into a young tiger. In the evenings they would climb down from their tower and explore their surroundings. The natural instincts of the tiger soon came to the front and it learnt to hunt and fend for itself. But, a peculiar bond was also forged between the girl and the beast. They became as shadows to each other.

Purity devised many vocal commands, gestures and whistles to which the beast readily responded. She also learnt to read the mind of the tiger by his demeanour and actions. On occasions, when they had wandered too far from their cave and it seemed that darkness might overtake them in the open, she would gesture to the tiger who would then crouch down and she would climb on its back. If any man or woman should see this sight of a magnificent silver tiger with a young girl on its back, bounding across the fields, they should surely believe that this was the stuff of legends.

Only once during the early weeks of her stay in the cave did she experience some anxiety concerning passing strangers. One evening as the tiger and she reposed on the ledge outside the cave, she observed a group of six men passing along the road. Suddenly they stopped and she saw them glancing towards the hill. There appeared to be an animated discussion between them and a number of them moved in her direction. Swiftly Purity moved into the shadow of the cave from where she could watch proceedings unobserved. One of the figures that had remained on the road ran after the others and with much gesturing and gesticulation implored them to return. After some time they did so, and went on their way. Purity breathed a sigh of relief.

Time passed and soon winter drew near. The days grew shorter and the nights longer and the cold winds that swept the plateau began to bite. Inside the cave it was warm and comfortable and Purity decided that they should stay where they were until the spring.

Will they live here undisturbed?

No, I don't think so, my angel.

What is going to happen to them?

Well, my darling, I believe time may spring a few surprises on them.

Go on, then! I can't wait!

✠

The end of the year and the middle of winter approached. The days were short and bleak and the nights long and cold. For this reason Purity and the tiger did not leave the cave in the evenings anymore. Instead, they would search for food during daylight hours. It was reasonably safe to do so, because at this time of year very few travellers moved along the track that crossed the plateau.

One day they arrived back at the cave in the late afternoon. It was the last day before the turn of the season. Purity had lit a small fire on the altar on which she was roasting a hare for her supper. The tiger was crouched in a corner, devouring a small deer. After they had finished their meal, they sat on the ledge outside the cave, but soon the fading light and the chill drove them inside. After a while she rolled herself in a rug and retired for the night with the tiger lying close and warm beside her.

It was as midnight approached that she was roused from her sleep. The first she noticed was that the tiger was also awake. It was staring at the entrance to the cave, its ears thrown back and pricked. At first she did not know what it was that woke her, but then she heard it again: there was the clink of metal and it sounded as if it came from the foot of the hill.

The cave itself was filled with a soft glow of light. Slowly and quietly she rose and gently parted a chink in the plant curtain. She realised that the light was coming from the full moon that was shining directly at the entrance of the cave. She looked down and her body became tense. The tiger moved to stand beside her and from the corner of her eye she saw the silver mane on its back rise.

Below her stood three figures, dressed in long white cloaks. The figure at the front had a sling around its neck from which was suspended an object which appeared to be a bowl or a jar. Slowly it moved away from the other two and made as if to climb the hill. She had to make a swift decision: should she confront the figure when it reached the entrance to the cave or should she make her presence known while there was still some distance between them. She decided on the latter.

She placed her hand on the tiger's neck, parted the curtain and the two of them stepped out onto the ledge and into the full glare of the moon. The figure that was climbing the hill was so intent on its task that it did not see them, but those at the foot of the hill saw the woman and the tiger emerging from the cave and cried out in startled alarm. The other looked up from its climb. She saw that he was a man. With a start he jerked upright, lost his footing and slithered back down the hill. Purity had not worn her hood when she emerged from the cave and, looking up, those at the foot of the hill saw a young woman with long blonde hair falling to her waist. And, standing next to her, the magnificent figure of the large silver cat. With many cries they all turned and ran away from the hill.

Purity decided that they had to leave at once. Their hiding place had been discovered and she realised that others would soon be back. Swiftly she gathered her belongings together and re-emerged onto the ledge and her heart sank. She saw that a horde of people was swarming towards them across the fields from the road in the distance. Those that were at the hill ran to meet them and after a brief and agitated conversation, they all swarmed towards the hill. Escape was impossible. By the time the tiger and she had made their descent the horde would be upon them. She knew that she would soon be captured, but at least she could defend herself for some time from her present site. They would have to climb the hill in order to reach her and although she knew that she would eventually be overwhelmed, she also knew that she could kill a number of them before this should happen.

She stepped back into the cave and dropped the plant curtain shut behind her. Then, she and the tiger crouched together. She picked up her bow and fitted an arrow onto the string.

And that, my darling, is where we will leave her for the present.

But, you can't do that! She may be in mortal danger!

That is possibly true, my little angel. But, we need to find out how the hunter is getting on. So, for the time being we will return to him and his friends. I also believe that it is time that we should pay another visit to the oracle and see what he has up his sleeve.

The hunter and the party of rescuers rode all night. Their first priority was to get as far away from the city as possible before the escape was discovered. They believed that the city guards would search the immediate vicinity of the city at the earliest opportunity, but that they would not be pursued until daylight. It was therefore essential that they should put as much distance between themselves and the city before the sun rose.

As the sun poked its head over the horizon, they decided to rest themselves and their horses for a short spell. The forest still laid quite some leagues away and they could not tardy for too long. After they had broken their fast they moved on.

Their immediate aim was to throw their pursuers off the scent. To this purpose they swept the tracks behind them at frequent intervals. Also, whenever they reached a stream, they would follow its course for some time before leaving it. All this consumed precious time, but they considered it worth their while.

They travelled until darkness fell and then decided to rest for the night. It was not wise to light a fire and so they dined on cold meat, bread and wine. Acting in turns as lookout and guard, they slept until dawn and then moved on.

Now another trouble beset them: their horses were not fresh and their progress became sluggish. At noon the following day the master builder's horse became so lame that it was unable to continue. The horse was let loose and the builder was mounted behind the doctor, but this slowed their progress even more since the one tired horse had to carry two people.

The forest was still some distance away when the master builder looked over his shoulder and saw a dust cloud behind them. Although they made as much haste as their tired horses would allow, the cloud of dust drew ever nearer and soon they could make out the figures of their pursuers. The enemy had been able to bring spare horses with them and, although the forest was looming ahead, they were closing in fast. Soon they could hear the jubilant shouts of the horde behind them and stray arrows began to fall all around.

The hunter decided that it would be prudent for them to split up, and for each man to make his own way into the forest. This action through the enemy into some confusion and it gave the companions some short respite. They spread out to left and right and raced for the forest, but the doctor's horse, having to carry two riders, fell behind. Suddenly the master builder's body jerked and at the same time the horse stumbled. Arrows had struck both the master builder and the horse. The horse fell and both the riders tumbled onto the earth. The doctor jumped to his feet and tried to raise his friend, but then saw with alarm that an arrow was protruding from his back.

One of the following riders had seen the horse falling and he rode ahead with a great cry of joy, intent on dealing the fatal blow to the two stricken riders. He stopped in front of them and, with a vicious grin of glee, he raised his sword high in the air, readying himself to bring it down with all his might on the doctor's head. The doctor prepared himself for death, but then he heard the twang of a bowstring behind him and, as if by magic, the shaft of an arrow was protruding from the swordsman's throat. With a look of surprise he dropped his sword and his hands flew to his throat. With blood gushing from his mouth, he frantically tried to wrench the arrow from his throat, but then he fell sideways off his horse onto the ground and was still.

The pursuing riders had seen their comrade falling and this halted them in their tracks. Suddenly, the hunter appeared next to the doctor and he raised their wounded colleague onto his shoulder. With a shout he commanded the doctor to follow him and they raced for the trees on the edge of the forest. The enemy had gathered themselves and was chasing hard, but the companions had now reached the trees and the safety of the forest.

Here, in this dark interior, the hunter was at home. Soon he had gathered the companions together and, urging them to flee deeper into the forest, he remained behind in order to cause further diversions. To this end he took some very fine snares from his cloak. These he tied between pairs of trees at different heights. Then he retreated deeper into the forest from where he observed the pursuers. In retreating he behaved intentionally clumsy and he made such a noise so that the queen's men had little option but to follow his trail. Thus he led them to the trap, which he had set for them. When they reached the snares, all were thrown into confusion. Horses stumbled over the snares and riders were cruelly wounded and dismounted. The hunter watched with satisfaction as a fine snare caught one of the front riders just below the chin. The snare cut through the throat and the flesh of his neck with such force that his head was removed from his body. The headless corpse continued for some distance, blood spurting high in the air, before it toppled sideways from the horse. Those riders who followed behind soon realised the danger ahead and they reigned their horses in, unwilling to continue with the pursuit. Swiftly the hunter and the companions made their escape into the forest.

As soon as they were safe, they stopped and the doctor examined their stricken companion. Fortunately, the arrow did not penetrate deeply and had missed all vital organs. Working swiftly and skilfully, he cut the arrow free and bound the wound. But, now, having to take care of their wounded friend, they were unable to make further progress. They decided to remain where they were until his wounds had healed.

And, my darling that is where we will leave them for a while.

Where shall we go next?

Let us go and find out what the nasty old queen is up to, shall we?

※

The escape of the hunter was discovered as soon as the guard was changed. At first they tried to revive the four sleeping men, but this proved to be impossible due to the drug that was administered to them. So, instead the miscreants were roughly carried back to the city where they were unceremoniously dumped into the dungeons. All through the night the doctors tried to rouse them, but the drug proved to be so strong that they remained lifeless until the following morning.

As soon as they returned to consciousness, the interrogators moved in and each man was questioned as to what happened during the night. At first, each man had a different tale to tell; one said that some elves had come to them during the night and had placed a spell on them. Another told of how the goddess of the hunt had come down from her abode in the sky and had spirited her subject away. The third man told a tale of a large snake appearing on the scene. Believing that the snake was about to devour the hunter, they had all moved closer in order to appreciate the sport. But, instead of savaging the hunter, the snake had turned its malevolent gaze upon the guards and charmed them into a deep sleep. The fourth guard told of a demon from the underworld that appeared to them. It threatened them with eternal damnation and fire if they did not let the hunter go. They were all so afraid that they fell into a stupor. Each tale was more fantastic than the other and, suffice it to say, none were believed.

The queen decided that she had little time to waste. She had to discover the truth before the prisoner got out of her reach. She therefore instructed the interrogators to call on the services of the torturers. These evil men arrived with there various instruments of fire, screws and racks and it did not take them long to extract the truth of what had happened from the four guards.

After all had been told, they were thrown back into the dungeon and left until the evening. At dusk they were removed to the tree of execution where they were stripped and tied and left for the attention of the animals. In their case the queen did not even afford them the benefit of a trial.

As soon as the truth was discovered, the queen dispatched a large troupe of men after the hunter and his rescuers. They took with them some experienced trackers and they also had the benefit of fresh, spare horses. These factors allowed them to make good ground on their escaping quarry. For two days they followed in the chase and on the eve of the second day, on the outskirts of the great forest, they caught up with them, but, alas, it was too late. The hunter and his companions had escaped their clutches.

With two dead men and many wounded, as well as the news of their failure they returned to the city. The queen was not pleased with their failure. In her paranoid mind she convinced herself that her men had acted against her. She accused them all of treachery and disloyalty and they were summarily executed.

Oh, dear! If she keeps on killing people off at this rate she is not going to have a lot of supporters left. Surely, most people in the city must realise by now just what an evil woman she is. Why don't they rebel against her?

Ah. if it was only that simple, my love. In my opinion the world can be roughly divided into two groups: Those who wish to rule and those who wish to be ruled. The second group is by far the larger and they consist mostly of peaceful cowards. Sometimes a leader or two may emerge from this second group, but if their ideas are not in tune with the rulers, they are easily neutralised. And, this is exactly what the queen did. She imposed a nightly curfew. None was allowed to walk the streets after sunset. Also, all those who plotted against her were soon sniffed out and either executed or banished. She surrounded herself with like-minded supporters; those who craved power at all cost. Gatherings of more than two people in public were forbidden and at night, none but the occupants of each house were allowed to be in residence. In short, all pretence of being a benign ruler had been discarded.

And now, my darling, we will pay a visit to the oracle.

※

"Will you take some wine with me, Father?"

"Ah, thank you, Oracle. That will be most pleasant.

The oracle pours some wine from a jug into two goblets.

"Let us not drink this wine as a toast, for there is not much that we can drink a toast to at present. Rather, let us think of it as a libation to the gods and let us entreat them to look favourably on us in our present troubles. So, first, let us drink to our deceased king who was a just and honourable man and who left us through the dishonour of others in the prime of his life. May the gods take his spirit from this world and raise him to their presence, there to sit with them in everlasting glory. Then, let us drink to our princess who is forced to wander alone in the wilderness. May the gods protect her from danger. Furthermore, let us drink to our people and our city that are borne down under an evil yoke. May this burden soon be lifted from them. And, finally, let us drink to the destruction of all evil. May the gods relieve us from these vipers in our midst and cast them into the underworld where they should suffer eternal fiery torment."

"Oracle, I get the distinct impression that you are rather angry."

"That I am, I fear. And with good reason. It angers me greatly to witness this evil that is inflicted on our city and on our people. In a strange way, what is worse is that this monster is not even of our own making. Like a maggot she has wriggled into our core. She is nothing but a vainglorious, conniving, power-hungry outsider. It fills me with grievous wonder to see what havoc this misfit has caused in such a short time."

"Oh, Oracle! You never cease to amaze me! Whenever I think that I know you, you manage to spring another surprise on me. I would never have accused you until now of being xenophobic. On the other hand, I do not know why it should surprise me. I have known for years that there is in fact a very human spirit hidden beneath that holy exterior that you present to your people."

"I am sorry for my outburst, Holy Father. Circumstances demand that I should be calm. In fact, calm thought is what is demanded from all of us in the temple. For the present we have escaped her attention and we should keep it like that. It is up to us to resolve this unpleasant situation."

"Have you ought in mind, Oracle?"

"I think so, Holy One. I believe that we should give it time until the next rising of the full moon to receive news from the hunter and his companions. If anyone should find our princess, the hunter will do so. It will take some time though, since she has a long head start on them."

"And, if no news comes? What then?"

"Then I will have to take matters into my own hands. I may have to leave here and search for her myself."

"That will indeed be unprecedented, Oracle. You know that you are not supposed to be seen in public. The gods may frown on such action."

"As I see it, High Priest, the gods are not exactly helpful at present. And, I believe that, if they are not going to be forthcoming with any assistance in our plight, we have no alternative but to help ourselves. Let us worry after the event about the anger of the gods. Their vengeance cannot be worse than our present situation. Anyway, if I should leave the temple, (as I have done before), I shall take great care that I am not recognised."

"Well, Oracle, you have always been right and I shall not question your actions on this occasion."

"Thank you, Holy Father. But, as I have already stated, let us keep our heads down for the present. We must take great care not to draw any attention to ourselves."

The high priest rises and, with a farewell greeting, leaves the room.

Do you think the oracle is right to be so concerned?

I believe he is, my angel.

But, what can he do about it? He is only a kind of priest, isn't he?

Oh, I think he will find a way. He is resourceful enough. Now, shall we return to Purity and see how she is getting on? Where did we leave her? Oh, yes. A horde of people is descending on her. It looks as if she may be trapped and caught in her cave.

Purity watched anxiously from behind her plant curtain as the crowd of men and women rushed towards her across the open plane. In her hands she held the bow and she had fitted an arrow onto the string. Next to her the tiger crouched. She could feel the protective warmth of its body against her flank. Soon the fastest runners in the crowd were within range of her arrows, but she decided to hold her fire. She would wait for them to climb the hill. She would not let an arrow go until the foremost reached the level of the ledge. She could not afford to miss. Also, a stricken body falling from the top of the hill would inevitably take some of those who followed with it.

In a furious rush the crowd reached the hill. And then, a most wondrous thing happened. Instead of rushing up the hill, the front-runners fell onto their faces. Soon the rest of their companions reached them and they also prostrated themselves. There were many scores of them. Purity looked in wonder at the scene below. The field in the vicinity of the hill was covered in bodies that lay as if mortally stricken. The moon glinted brightly on the white cloaks that they all appeared to be dressed in. The scene was captured, motionless and still as if in a frieze.

Then, a movement caught her eye. An old man near the front of the prostrated horde first raised his head and then came cautiously to his knees. Slowly he crawled towards the base of the hill and, on reaching it he raised his arms as if in supplication and spoke thus:

"Oh, Goddess of the Harvest! Alas, the prophecy has come true! We, Your people, greet You! For countless moons we have waited for this glorious day when You might appear amongst us! Our hearts and our minds overflow with joy! Blessed be the day! Will You not reveal Your own presence to us? Will You not bestow Your blessing upon us? Will You not come forth so that we may look upon Your countenance? Will You accept our meagre offering and will You bless the fields and all its fruits?" So saying, He brought forth two small jars from his ample cloak: One containing corn and one wine. With this all the people rose to their knees and produced similar containers and, as one, they made a libation on the earth.

Purity was at a loss as to what to do. Should she show herself or should she remain concealed? Surely, eventually she had to face them. Should she disillusion them as to her person? But, if she did so they would most certainly kill her. For, did she not invade an obviously sacred place? She pondered upon her precarious situation for a while and then she made her decision. For the present she would take on the role of Goddess of the Harvest. Once she was away from the hill and the cave, she could re-consider her position and plan appropriately. She rose to her feet and, with the tiger beside her she parted the plant curtain and stepped onto the ledge.

As she faced the crowd, she raised her arms and stretched her hands towards them in blessing. The air was filled by sibilance. At first she thought that it was the sound of the wind, but then she realised that the air around her was still and that the sound came from the people. As one they had released the breath in their lungs in a sigh of relief and joy. But, now she was faced by another problem: Should she address the crowd and, if so, what should she say to them? Swiftly she made her decision: She would remain silent and aloof. She would behave with the quiet dignity of a goddess.

Purity gestured to the tiger and with alacrity it bounded down the hill. With a cry of alarm the crowd retreated from the beast, but as it reached the foot of the hill, the tiger turned its gaze on its mistress and waited for her to descend the hill. With as much dignity as she could muster, she climbed down from the ledge and took her place next to the beast. A silence fell over the crowd and soon she realised that they were waiting for her to speak or act. Apparently without signal, the tiger stepped in front of her and crouched and, to the astonishment of all, she climbed upon its back. As she moved towards them, they parted and she entered their midst. Then they all moved away from the hill and proceeded towards the road in the distance.

At first all was silent, but soon a soft murmur broke out amongst the crowd. Gradually they moved closer and with awe in their eyes they began to touch her hair and the flanks of the tiger. Now there was no doubt in their minds: Surely, only a goddess could be as fair as this? And, only a goddess could tame and befriend the silver tiger, that most vicious of all animals?

After some time the elder who had addressed her earlier stepped forward and spoke to her again:

"Oh, Goddess of the Harvest. We entreat You to accompany us to our humble village. Will You not bring glory upon us, Your people, by your presence? We beg of You that You should stay with us until the summer harvest."

Silently she assented to his request and with great joy and much singing the crowd directed her and the tiger towards their settlement.

I believe that our princess has just jumped out of the frying pan into the fire.

Now, why should you think that, my angel?

Surely, she could not sustain this illusion of a goddess for too long, could she? Surely, she will soon be discovered?

Well, if so, let's hope that her resourcefulness stands her in good stead.

Are we staying with her for a bit longer?

No. Let's leave her for a while and see how the hunter is getting on.

The hunter and the companions moved some leagues into the great forest until they were certain that they had lost their pursuers. Here they rested and tended to their stricken friend. The doctor cut the arrow free and after applying some ointments, he bandaged the wound. Although the arrow did not strike any vital organs, the wound was deep enough and the patient could not be moved for some time. They therefore decided to stay where they were until their friend was healed. It was while they were thus occupied that another joined their party.

One day, while the hunter was out of camp and searching for provisions, he spied a man, travelling through the forest and leading a pony behind him. He instantly realised that the pony was lame and he also recognised the man. Like the hunter, he was a man who liked to travel widely and they had often met each other in distant places. After they had embraced, the man told his story:

He had entered the city some two moons ago, but he had found circumstances there much changed. The city had lost its joyful countenance and the mood was sombre. To crown everything, trade was bad. The quality of the goods was poor. He had therefore decided to leave the city and return to his own land. He had left the city the day after the hunter had made his escape. He told of the torture and punishment of the guards. The cruel and unjust events of the past week had sickened him to his soul and he had reached the conclusion that this city was no longer a place of peace and justice.

The hunter invited him to join their company and the traveller accepted. Initially he decided to stay only until such time as his pony's lameness had been cured, but he ultimately remained with them until the companion's wound had healed. After this he accompanied them on their journey. They told him about their quest to find the princess, Purity and he readily agreed to help them in their search. He was no slave to time and he had no urgent business any other place.

They did not linger in the forest for long, since the hunter realised that Purity would not be found there. He had left her in the forests edge near the plain between the steep hills and the forest and directed her towards the land of the canyon dwellers. He had no reason to believe that she would make her way back to the forest. They therefore made haste and a few days later they left this dark place and made their way onto the great plain. Here their search became more careful. They questioned many passing travellers and frequently they would stop at villages along the way to quiz the local population, but none had seen her. The hunter was not totally surprised, because, had he not instructed her to proceed with care? He had urged on her the need to wear a disguise at all times and not to let others know that she was a woman.

After some weeks they left the plain and entered the range of hills to the south. Here they made faster progress than Purity did, for they knew their way amongst the many paths that led into and up the steep hills. Eventually they reached the ravine where they decided to camp for the night. It was while the hunter was collecting firewood that he rounded an outcrop of rocks and found the remains of the silver tiger. The bones had been picked clean by carrion and the skeleton gleamed bright in the afternoon sun. Only a strip of mane remained by which the skeleton could be identified. The hunter moved in closer to see if he could determine the cause of the tiger's death. At first he was mystified, but then, as he parted the mane of the tiger, he saw the protruding blade and he recognised it immediately. With great excitement he called to the others. All gathered round to look in awe at the stricken beast.

Then one of the companions, the rather pessimistic master builder, voiced a thought: surely, it was beyond a mere girl to kill a great beast such as this? It was inevitable that she must also have perished in the struggle. But, although they searched the surrounding area extensively, they could find no sign of human remains and the hunter voiced the more optimistic thought that the girl had indeed killed the tiger and had come away unharmed. This, at least, was proof that they were on the right trail.

So, with strengthened hope in their hearts, they crossed the ravine on the following day. Since they had some horses and a pony, it was more difficult, but with much care they eventually reach the opposite side of the ravine. They continued along the wide road and made their way through and over the hills until they reached the valleys on the other side. Here, as on the plains, they visited settlements where they asked after the girl, but, once again, without any success.

In the autumn they neared the settlement that was home to their companion, the traveller. He invited them to stay at his house for a few days before continuing on their journey and they made their approach in the late afternoon. They climbed out of a deep valley and reached a plateau across which the road stretched. To the left of the road the hunter observed a hill and he commented on its strange, tower-like shape. He immediately veered off the road with the intention of examining the hill at closer quarters, but he was anxiously constrained by the traveller who entreated him not to approach the hill. He claimed that the hill and its surrounds were sacred. He told them that this was the dwelling of their goddess of the harvest. Only on the night of midwinter were mortals permitted near this place so that they could sacrifice to her and ask for her blessing of the next summer's harvest. Reluctantly, the hunter submitted to his entreaties and returned to the road. Swiftly they moved on and by nightfall they reached the settlement where they remained for a number of days.

This was indeed a respite that was sorely needed and welcomed by all the companions. They had been travelling and searching for a long time and they were more tired than they realised. When they had made their escape from the city, they had taken only a few articles of clothing with them and these were now worn and ragged. During their travels they had also relied on meat and fruit and roots from the forests and plains and they were hankering after fresh bread and milk to supplement their diet. It was therefore with alacrity that they accepted the invitation of the traveller to share the hospitality of his people.

They found these folk much to their liking. They were of a gentle disposition. Although they kept some goats in a communal herd, they ate meat but sparingly and they relied on the animals mainly for milk and cheese. They were a folk who bonded closely with the earth and, as well as the animal products, they ate wholesomely of the fruits and grains which they grew. Being late autumn, the harvest had been gathered in and stored and the village was largely at rest from daily toil. The hunter and the companions were invited to rest and to eat their fill. They were also provided with fine woollen cloth which they stitched into new breeches and cloaks or which they used to repair their old clothing.

On leaving the settlement, they travelled south across the remaining valleys, always enquiring after the princess, but still without any success. On and on they travelled and the aspect of the surrounding countryside became wild and mountainous. Eventually, after travelling for many weeks, they came to an area where the land sloped upwards. Although the incline stretched for many leagues, it was not steep and for two days they made their way onwards and upwards until, suddenly, they reached the top and they beheld a most magnificent sight.

In front of them the ground fell away steeply into the base of a very large canyon. Just visible in the far distance, was the opposite wall of the canyon. Far, far below them the sun glinted off a wide, smooth-flowing river. And, on either bank they saw movement as of scurrying ants. This, they realised, were the people and animals that inhabited this deep place. The cliff faces that formed the walls dropped steeply away and were covered in dense foliage of red, green and yellow. High on the cliffs they could see the nests of large birds and eagles and falcons could be seen floating and diving through the still air. They had reached the land of the Canyon-Dwellers.

They had all been to this land before and this sight was familiar to them, but they were still filled with feelings of wonder. Looking down on the scene, they experienced a great sense of awe at the vastness of what stretched before them and at the same time their spirits were suffused with a great feeling of peace.

Suddenly, they found themselves to be surrounded by a group of heavily armed men dressed in uniforms of green shirts and tunics. Looking to either side they could now see the two fortresses that guarded the road to the canyon. These were some of the soldiers that manned the fortresses.

The four companions were totally unperturbed and they greeted the soldiers heartily. In their turn the soldiers, having recognised the companions, lowered their arms and they all embraced. After the hunter and the traveller had been introduced, they were taken to one of the fortresses where they were fed and where they rested for a short while.

Purity

In the late afternoon they made their way down the steep slope of the canyon and that same night they slept in the house of the doctor.

It sounds rather magnificent, this land of the canyon dwellers. Who rules over it?

I don't know yet, my little angel. I have to think about it. Remember, I am making this story up as I go along. But, for the moment we will leave the hunter, the traveller and the companions in peace. Let them have a little rest. Instead, we will find out how Purity is getting on. I think there may be some trouble ahead for her.

※

The princess lives in the village with the people who had discovered her in the cave. She remains silent. She is provided with all the necessities for a comfortable existence: clothing of the best that this poor village can afford, food, drink and a comfortable dwelling. She is treated with the reverence afforded to a goddess. This disturbs her. She experiences guilt due to the fact that she, through necessity, has to deceive these kind and honest people. She is not required to perform any duties in the settlement, but she makes it clear that she wishes to contribute. The people of the village are farmers of grains and fruit. They are not natural hunters. Every day she leaves the village with the tiger and by evening she returns with deer which she presents to the village folk.

Why does she not escape? She is not held captive. She had been uprooted from a life where she had the constant companionship of others. For more than half a year she had no opportunity to converse with others. She enjoys the simple company of these people. True, she does not speak to them, but there is human contact and communication. She is loath to leave.

Spring arrives, glorious and mild and she helps with the planting. The people are happy. Surely, if the goddess lends a hand with the planting, the harvest will be good.

Then, two events occur that will shape her immediate future. The first concerns the tiger. With the coming of spring, she notices restlessness in the animal. At night it would leave her side, at first just for short periods, but with each night these periods of absence would last longer and longer. And, then, one day, the tiger does not return. Although she grieves for the loss of the tiger, she is philosophical about it. She realises that the noble beast had no other option and that it was purely responding to the call of nature. Maybe this was a sign from the gods that she also should move on.

Then, in late spring, the second event occurs: A man rides into the village on a steed. Although a man of the village, he is unique, for he is also a traveller. He is welcomed with joy and there is much conversation. He is told about the goddess in their midst and he is keen to meet her. When she returns from the fields in the evening, he sees her and a thoughtful look crosses his eyes. He makes some more enquiries: Who found her? Where was she discovered? How long had she been in the village? After all his queries had been answered, he ponders some more. Then, he comes to a decision. He requests a meeting with the elders.

The elders convene in the great, round hut in the centre of the village. The traveller enters and bows to the elders. The chief of the elders acknowledges his greeting and beckons him to take a seat within their circle. He speaks:

"Welcome, Friend! Welcome" Take your ease and tell us your news! Did you travel far this time?"

"Indeed, Father. I have travelled far and wide and I have seen much."

"Did you call this meeting to tell us about your travels? Come, friend. Tell us about the many roads you have traversed and all those wondrous things you have encountered on their routes."

"It is my opinion that there is but one road, and this road starts at the door of my dwelling. As every leaf, every twig, every branch is part of the same trunk of a tree, so every track and every path is a part of the great road of life. As I set foot outside my abode each morning, I think of it as the first step on that vast road of opportunity. But, enough of this philosophising. To return to your request: No, Father. For that I will wait until the next feast when all the folk will be gathered. I might as well bore everybody to sleep at once."

"No, my friend. Your tales are never boring. We would all like to travel like you, but, alas, I am afraid we are all too idle. You are our ears and our eyes and we crave for news from the outside world. So, then. Tell me. What is it that you wish to see the council about?"

"I have a strange tale to tell: A tale that affects this village particularly."

"Indeed! The world has finally encroached on this humble village? Come, Friend! Tell all!"

"This may take some time to tell and I crave your indulgence."

"Go on, Man! Tell us that which is on your mind!"

"Some two years ago I lived in a city far to the north. It was a very good city to live in. It is a place that is well known for its silver mines and its silver products. The people are all prosperous and the trade is always good."

"This city sounds too good to be true."

"Yes, indeed, Father. But, that is not all. Over this city ruled a king. This king was a kind and generous man who loved his subjects and his subjects returned his love. The king took a fair and gentle lady for his queen and she bore him a child, a beautiful princess. But, alas, the queen died with the birth of the princess. After some time the king married again. This time he took for his queen a dark lady. She was not only dark in countenance, but also in spirit. A most ambitious lady, she wished to be the sole ruler of the city. She was also very jealous of the young princess who was not only adored by the king, but also by his subjects. Eventually, the king died and it is rumoured that he was murdered by his dark queen. Then, it is told, she attempted to rid herself of the princess. She employed a hunter and instructed him to take the princess into the forest where he should dispose of her. However, the hunter fell under the spell of the princess and he allowed her to escape. The queen, discovering the treachery of the hunter, determined to put him to death, but he managed to escape. On leaving the princess, the hunter instructed her to make her way to the land of the canyon dwellers."

"So, how does all this affect us?"

"Have patience with me, Father. I will tell you all. Although the city is now ruled with the iron hand of the dark queen, there are some people of influence who would like to discover the whereabouts of the princess and bring her back. The hunter's escape was effected by these people and he was instructed to go in search of the princess. As I travelled south, I stumbled across the hunter and his companions and for many months we have been searching for her, but without success. Eventually, we reached the land of the canyon dwellers where I left them. On reaching the village today, I am told that there is a goddess in our midst and this afternoon I set eyes on her. I am afraid, Father, that she is no goddess. Unless I am badly mistaken, I believe that the lady who is living in our village is none other than the princess, Purity."

"This is indeed grave tidings you bring, Friend. As a man of peace and justice, my heart goes out to her, but she must answer for the trespasses she committed. I suggest we bring her into our midst and let her make her own defence."

One of the council is dispatched to fetch her.

Earlier that day, Purity notices the stranger in the settlement and she is also aware of the glances he directs towards her. She also becomes aware of the gathering of the council. She feels uneasy and cautiously, without any-one noticing, she makes her way to the back of the council hut and listens. Very soon her unease turns to disquiet and alarm. She does not need to hear too much to know that she had been discovered for what she was. With a heavy heart she realises that she has no option but to leave this place of comfort and kindness. Her heart is filled with guilt and remorse. She could not blame these kind and generous people if they should view her actions as a gross betrayal of their trust. With hindsight she realises that it would have been better for all if she had told the truth. But, alas, it was too late now. She has no option but to flee from this place.

Hastily, she returns to her own hut, gathers her belongings and, in the twilight she leaves unobserved.

The council member returns:

"I am afraid the girl has left. All her belongings have gone and the hut is empty."

"This is not good news. This calls for discussion and careful thought."

After some discussion, the council decides to call a meeting of the whole village. After the crimes that had been committed it is deemed right that all should have a say in what course of action should be taken.

Surely, she did not do anything so very terrible, did she?

Well, my darling, she only invaded the sacred cave of the harvest goddess and then posed as her. Remember, these are a simple folk and these things mean a lot to them. They could not let it go unpunished.

At least she managed to escape. There is not a lot they can do to her.

Let us find out, my little angel.

A number of the council members are dispatched and all the villagers are gathered in the square. Those who are still working in the fields are urged to leave their unfinished tasks and to join the rest.

The leader of the council speaks and relates the tale of the traveller. The gathering cries out in amazement and horror at the tale. The councillor concludes:

"Before we decide on what action should be taken concerning the girl, we have to determine whether any amongst us should be held responsible for what has happened. Two questions need to be answered: How long did she live in the sacred cave? And, Why was she not discovered earlier? Who amongst you was charged with tending to the goddess?"

A frail man steps forward:

"I was, Father."

"On every fourteenth day it is your duty to take an offering to the goddess on behalf of the tribe. Did you not on these occasions encounter the girl?"

The frail man becomes uneasy:

"I have not been well, Father. The climb to the cave is difficult and I am an old man. I know that the goddess will have patience with me so, will you not show me mercy?"

"Come, come now, old man! Tell the truth! Have you entered the cave since the beginning of winter?"

The old man quails:

"It is a long way to the cave! (He coughs), "I have been unwell for many a moon! But, I will make amends! Just tell me what to do!

"You will leave this village on the morrow. You will take your belongings with you and you will travel to the sacred hill. There you will stay for six moons and you will make daily sacrifices to the goddess.

"This will surely kill me!

"Then, so be it. If you should survive this ordeal you may return to the village, for it will be a sign that the goddess has seen fit to forgive your crime. Away with you! Now, what is to be done about the girl?"

More discussions follow. Some believe that the girl should be sought out and punished. Others, especially the young men, urge leniency. Then, a wise old man stands and speaks thus:

"Surely, the girl cannot be blamed for entering and living in the sacred cave? If there was no offering in the cave to indicate its purpose, how was she to know that she was trespassing? And, has she not behaved with dignity and gentleness whilst in our midst? Did she not always labour as hard as any other in this village? Did she not always show respect and gentle kindness to any who crossed her path? Has she not been treated most vilely by her own kinsmen? And, is it not a miracle in itself that she endured all that has happened to her? I say that she is favoured by the gods and that we should find her and return her to the bosom of her friends."

Some debate follows and then a vote is taken. The old man's eloquence has swayed them to his way of thinking and his proposal is accepted. The traveller is charged with the duty of finding her and escorting her to the land of the Canyon-Dwellers.

If the hunter and his companions could not find the princess, how is the traveller going to manage? I have a feeling that our girl is going to be stuck in the wilderness forever!

You are right, my love. It will have to be a matter of luck rather than good planning and judgement to catch up with her. But, don't despair! Let us continue.

Purity left the settlement as dusk was falling. Fortunately, she knew the surrounding area well due to the fact that she was not confined to the village during her stay and she swiftly made her way back to the road that crossed the plateau. On reaching the road she turned south and started her long walk through the night. She realised that her absence would soon be discovered and that it was imperative that she put as much distance as possible between herself and the village. There was no doubt in her mind that they would pursue her.

At sunrise the next morning, she decided to rest. She turned off the road and entered a small thicket where she took shelter. She drank some water and slept until early noon. Then she continued on her way until nightfall. Once again she rested for only a short while. For five days she continued in this fashion, living off the fruit and berries of the field and drinking from an occasional spring on her way.

On the sixth day she shot a hare which she skinned and from which she stripped the meat. This she half dried in the sun and ate before continuing on her relentless way.

On the seventh day two things happened: the first was that the road came to a sudden end. The terrain was now hilly and wild and she had no idea as to which direction to go. Aimlessly she wandered along the many rough tracks that wound amongst the many hills and soon she realised that she was totally lost.

The second thing that happened was that she had the feeling of being followed. This feeling was born purely out of intuition. She would frequently stop and look behind her, but she was always alone. However, this awareness grew steadily stronger as the day progressed.

As night fell she crawled into a dense thicket for shelter. She rolled herself in a rug and tried to sleep, but none would come. Her mind was filled with too much anxiety. Now, for the first time since she had been cast out of her home, she was overcome by despair. She was so utterly alone in this world. It seemed that she was destined to wander aimlessly and in solitude for the rest of her existence. What kind of a life was this to lead? Was it worth continuing with this struggle? These and many other questions filled her mind as she stared glumly into the darkness.

Then, a most strange thing happened: she was certain that she was not asleep, for she could feel the hard earth underneath her where she was lying and she was aware of the cool air of the night on her face. From some distance away in the woods, a faint white light materialised, but strangely, she was not afraid. The light rapidly approached her and grew in intensity. Out of the night a horseman on a great, white steed materialised and she saw that the light was emanating from his being. She instantly recognised the man for who he was: Her Father, the dead king. As he reached where she lay, he reigned in his horse and looked down on her. She noted that his approach was completely silent. The horse's hooves made no sound on the stony earth. He spoke:

"What ails thee, my daughter?"

"Oh, my father! I am so alone. I am confined in a world where I have become a fugitive. I am so tired of fleeing from all. I do not wish to wander endlessly anymore. I hanker for days gone by: for those simple things I used to take for granted; a walk in the park at sunset, the smell of fresh cut meadows, to wear a pretty dress again, to swim and splash with my friends in the great pool in the palace courtyard. All these things are now lost to me and I am destined for an endless life of toil and fear. Oh, my father! I have no desire for this! Please take me away to that place where you abide. I do not know what I might find there, but surely, it will be better than this harsh world and I will be by your side again."

The king looked down on her with a sorrowful smile: "Do not despair so, my child. All is not lost. When you were born your mother gave you into my safe keeping. Whilst I was in your world I protected you with my body and my sword and my counsel. But, do not be afraid. From where I am now I still keep a keen eye on you. It is written in the book of your birth that you are destined for greatness. Have courage, my daughter. Have courage. I know that the gods look on you with favour and with their help I will protect you."

So saying, he turned his steed around and, surrounded by the light, he faded back into the woods from whence he came. And Purity felt strong and at peace.

Then she was shaken from her reverie. She had suddenly become aware of her surroundings. The night air around her was silent as an enclosed tomb. It was too quiet. There was no sound of night bird or cricket or, indeed, even of the little creatures that scurry and rustle in the undergrowth. Then she heard it and her body tensed. A loud "crack" shattered the silence and she instinctively knew what it was: A large creature, either man or beast, had stepped on a twig and broken it under foot.

Quietly, and with a new resolution born out of the vision, she rose from her bed and crouched with her back against a tree, facing in the direction of the disturbance. Across her lap she held her bow, an arrow fitted to the string. Thus she sat for some considerable time and nothing happened. After a while she began to wonder if her imagination may be playing tricks on her, but then she listened once more to the silence that surrounded her and she was certain that something or somebody was afoot. Whatever it was had produced a caution amongst the creatures of the night.

She jumped with alarm as the voice came to her from no more than ten paces to her right:

"Princess Purity," it said quietly. "Be not afraid, for I come in peace."

"Who are you?"" She also spoke in hushed tones.

"I am a traveller that hails from the settlement where you spent the winter months. I arrived on the night that you took flight."

"I remember you. You went to speak to the council about me. That is why I took flight. And, what should you want with me?"

"I have come to offer assistance."

"Why should I believe you? You denounced me to the council. How could I be certain that you would not kill me or take me back to your people? Did I not desecrate the abode of your goddess and did I not impersonate her? I should be very foolish if I were to believe that these crimes would not be viewed in a serious light by your folk."

"The crimes were indeed serious. But, tell me princess: How much did you hear of our conversation?"

"Enough to know that I was in severe trouble."

"Then, you did not hear me tell them of the circumstances that were the cause of your misfortune? You also did not hear me tell of what befell the hunter?"

"Where is the hunter? What has happened to him?"

Swiftly and in brief he told her all that had happened to the hunter: his betrayal, his imprisonment and his rescue and escape. He also told her of the mission that he had been charged with: to find her and care for her until such time as the dark queen could be overthrown and Purity could be restored to the throne.

"A vote was taken amongst my people and it was decided that your crimes were inadvertently committed. You have been absolved. I, in turn, have been charged with finding you and to take you to the hunter. He is residing with the canyon dwellers."

Purity realised that she had little option but to accept what the traveller told as the truth and she invited him into the clearing. All that night they talked. She asked him many questions concerning her city and he told all he knew.

The next day they continued on their journey. Although she maintained her disguise, she could now travel without anxiety. She felt at peace and secure under the protection of the stranger.

Eventually, after many weeks, they reached the long incline that led to the canyon. Here they decided to rest for the night before making the long ascent.

After taking their evening meal, they talked for a while and then rolled themselves in their rugs. But, that night sleep did not come easily to the girl. She felt unaccountably restless and disturbed. She thought that it might be due to the fact that she was soon to be re-united with the hunter, a direct link with her past. Eventually, however, sleep did come, but even her dreams were troublesome.

She dreamt that she was lying on the grass in one of the beautiful parks of the city. Next to her was the silver tiger. She could feel the heat of his body against her skin. Above her stood her father. Strangely, she knew that he was not real, but that he was dead. His handsome face contained a sad smile. In his left hand he held an apple and in his right a little, sharp dagger. He was slicing pieces of apple and feeding it to the tiger. He spoke to her:

"Do not fear, my child. Be at peace. I know that I have been murdered by my wife and that you have been exiled by her, but there are many who have your welfare at heart. They will take care of you. Just keep faith and be strong. One day soon, you will be restored to the throne and all this beautiful city will be yours again. And, when that happens, make sure that you are generous in your rule." He had finished slicing the apple and he cleansed the knife by sticking it into the ground and withdrawing it. "And, now, I must return to my world. But, take courage, my little princess. I will never be far away."

Speaking thus, he turned and strolled away until he disappeared behind some trees.

The woman stirs. She does have some strange dreams, our Purity, does she not? First she dreamt that she was being chased and that she fell into the underworld, then she dreamt that she saw her father on a white horse and that he gave her guidance; and now she dreams that he is talking to her whilst feeding a tiger. Do you believe in dreams? Do you believe that they are symbolic of something else?

Personally I don't, my darling. I believe that, when we are asleep our subconscious comes to the fore and somehow reflect our fears, desires and pleasures. There are those, such as Sigmund Freud, who advocate that dreams have deeper symbolic meaning, but frankly I cannot see it.

I'll tell you what intrigues me about Herr Freud: as far as I understand it, he reached his conclusions on the human psyche after observing the behaviour and thoughts of a bunch of middle class Swiss women. Not very representative of the human race, is it my petal. It is a bit like doing market research in order to find out how popular bread is and then interviewing ten thousand wheat farmers.

You may be right. Anyway, please continue.

Purity awoke and found that she was crying. She felt so utterly alone. It was all so vivid. She could still see her father's gentle face and she could still feel the heat of the silver tiger by her side. She put out her hand to stroke the creature and then she jerked wide awake. She was touching the warm fur of an animal. She turned her head and she cried out with joy. The silver tiger had returned to her. She threw her arms about his neck and he licked her face with a furry tongue.

The traveller had come awake with the commotion and at first he was filled with alarm. He snatched his dagger from his belt and rushed at the animal. He believed that the princess was being mauled by the creature. With a warning shout she stopped him in his track and then he stared in wonder. He had heard from his people about this strange union between the girl and a silver tiger, but he had not quite believed it. They were but simple folk and he had assumed that it was all a figment of their imagination. But, now he had to believe his own eyes. The girl was embracing the tiger and it was licking her face. This wild, untameable beast might as well have been a domestic kitten.

Purity beckoned him to come nearer and she spoke quietly to the big cat. She urged the traveller to place his hand upon the tiger's neck. At first he was filled with anxiety, but with some gentle coaxing he eventually rested his hand on the tiger's neck and he felt the smooth, silky fur under his fingers and his mind was filled with awe of the beast and of the girl.

For the next two days they travelled up the gentle slope to the canyon and they reached their destination on the eve of the second day. Their arrival caused much commotion amongst the guards at the fortresses, but their anxieties were soon quelled. They had heard some talk of this princess down in the canyon, but now that they had met her, they looked in wonder at her beauty and they fell under her spell. The presence of the tiger enhanced her status amongst them and their demeanour towards her was more as of a goddess rather than a mere mortal.

That night they rested in one of the fortresses and the next day they made their descent into the canyon. Here, at last, she was re-united with the hunter and she also met the companions for the first time. At last, after a long year in the wilderness, she was amongst friends. She was not alone anymore. She was out of the wilderness.

And now, my little angel, we will have a little rest.

Will she get back to the city?

I don't know, my darling. I'll have to think about it.

She will need a lot of help.

I know. And, at this stage I am not so sure where this help is going to come from. But, as I said: Let us have a little rest, my beauty. I am sure inspiration will come.

Part 3: Return.

"It is the bright day that brings forth the adder and that craves wary walking."

William Shakespeare: "Julius Caesar"

Well now, my darling. We have reached the third part of our tale. Shall we have a précis of what has happened so far?

Why not?

Right, then. At the end of part one we left Purity alone in the wilderness. In part two the hunter returns to the city and declares her dead. Purity wanders through the wilderness and one day she encounters a stranger who wants to rape her. She fights him off and he turns up in the city and tells his tale. One of the queen's lackeys overhears him and recognises his description of Purity. He informs the dark queen and she realises that the hunter had deceived her. She condemns him to death, but he manages to escape with the help of the oracle and the companions. He is charged with the duty of finding the princess and protecting her. The city falls into decline.

Purity continues on her wandering. She reaches a ravine which, at first, appears to be impossible to cross. Here she finds a silver tiger cub which is trapped behind a rock-fall. Whilst trying to rescue the cub, she is attacked by its mother, but she manages to kill it. The tiger-cub becomes her friend and faithful companion.

Eventually she stumbles upon a cave on a hill where she finds shelter for herself and the tiger. Unbeknown to her, it is the temple of a local goddess. She is discovered by the folk who worship this deity, but she pretends to be the goddess. She is taken into the care of the people of the settlement, and she dwells with them for the winter.

Whilst searching for the princess, the hunter and the companions are joined by a traveller. It just so happens that this traveller comes from the village where Purity is sheltering. Unsuccessful in their search, the hunter, the companions and the traveller eventually reach the land of the Canyon-Dwellers. The hunter and the companions remain here while the traveller returns to his people.

On reaching his village, the traveller discovers Purity and informs the council. Purity realises the danger that she is in and she makes her escape. In her absence, the council and the people of the settlement pardon her and the traveller is sent after her and charged with the duty of finding her and re-uniting her with the hunter and the companions.

This he does and after finding her, they make their way towards the land of the Canyon-Dwellers. On their way the silver tiger, (who had left her for the wild during the winter), returns to her. After a year in exile, she rejoins the hunter and the companions in the land of the Canyon-Dwellers.

Is that a fair summary, my beauty?

Not bad. Now, where do we go from here?

I think it is about time we had another look at the state of mind of the dark queen and find out what she is getting up to; don't you think so, my angel?

Yes. Let's.

※

Two years had passed since the king's death and the procurement of the throne by the dark queen. The city was in spiritual decline. Those who wept for its impending death, did so in silence, for they knew that to do so with outward emotion, would result in pointless retribution. The city and its people were borne down under a most evil yoke. Where once there was joy, there was now only sorrow. Where once there was prosperity, there was now only poverty and hunger. The city was firmly in the grasp of her who was consumed by an obsessive lust for power.

Power. What is power. Power manifests itself in many different ways.

For example, the athlete treats power as a trial of strength. His aim is to hit harder, throw further or run faster than his opponent. Although his ambition is to be faster and stronger than others, he is never envious. Instead, he has the utmost respect for the power of other competitors and it spurs him on to achieve as much, if not more, than them.

Then there are those who possess power without even being aware of this fact. You belong to this category, my angel. Your power lies in your innocence. Both men and women wilt before your good nature. Because you are generous in your dealings with others, you have the world at your feet.

Then there are those who have an obsessive need of power. They are inward looking and selfish. Their main aim in this life is to dominate. And, with this desperate need comes a dread of failure. They live in a constant state of anxiety and paranoia. But, you know something, my darling: these people are totally unaware of the fact that they are obsessed. They lose touch with reality. Somehow they expect others to view them in the same light as they view themselves. They expect others to love, envy and admire them as they love, envy and admire themselves.

To this third category the dark queen belonged. With each passing day her lust for power and her vanity grew and she began to see all around her as a threat. Anyone who she suspected of opposing her, (mostly without good reason), she disposed of. She severed all alliances with surrounding cities and she fortified her own city against imaginary attacks.

The guard around the palace was strengthened and she seldom ventured outside. On the odd occasion when she did leave the palace, she surrounded herself with heavily armed men on horseback. When this happened, the people of the city stayed indoors, for they feared, hated and despised the queen. The city and its people had become entrenched.

The dark queen was fully aware of the hatred the people bore her and this filled her with an illogical fury. When she realised that she could not win their love and respect, she was determined to make them live in fear of her. She was fully aware of the feelings that the people still extended towards their long dead king and towards the princess and this infuriated her beyond measure. If she could not have their love, then she would ensure that they cowered before her and respected her power. To this end she persecuted them mercilessly. All public portraits of the king and Purity were removed and destroyed. If anyone was discovered to carry an image of the king or the princess on their person or kept it in their home, they would suffer severe punishment. The statue of the king that stood at the palace gate was taken down, broken into many pieces and cast outside the city walls. She would frequently instruct her guards to empty the market square and destroy the market stalls. The taverns would often be raided and many city folk would be arrested on trumped-up charges of treason. Whereas the tree of execution was formerly used as a place of retribution for crimes against the city, it was now employed as a site of entertainment for her soldiers.

Unlike the days when the king ruled and all stood graceful and glistening and proud, the city and its people were now brought to its knees. Most folk were poverty stricken and many diseases spread unchecked.

Those who owned the land outside the city walls were dispossessed and their property divided amongst the queen's closest friends. These were men and women who were nearly as crazed for power as the queen. Perversely, although these were the people who were her closest allies, deep within her soul she feared and distrusted them most. She recognised in them the qualities of her own nature.

The once prosperous silver mines had largely fallen into disuse. Only a very few were left open and the produce from these were horded by the queen and her followers. In short: The city was being raped and thousands of its old guard, soldiers and inhabitants were needlessly and brutally slaughtered.

This, then, was the domain that the dark queen created for herself.

There was, however, one matter that gnawed at the queen's mind like an indestructible maggot. It was the survival of Purity. However much she tried to convince herself that the princess was of no importance or no threat to herself, she could not banish her from her twisted mind. In her heart she knew that the folk of the city still grieved for the loss of Purity. Rumour had come to her ears that many people had created images in their homes of the princess. She therefore believed that it was imperative that Purity should be sought out and destroyed forever.

Single-minded as the dark queen was in her lust for power, let us not forget that she was not a stupid woman, my darling. She also had her spies who she sent out to roam the lands beyond the city. These spies were charged with the duty of bringing her news of the whereabouts of the princess. Many brought false news in order to keep favour with the queen, but with time she managed to sieve the false from the truth and in time she discovered that Purity was living in the land of the Canyon-Dwellers.

Another fact that the queen was ever aware of, but that she could not act upon until the present, was that the hunter's escape and the survival of the princess was largely due to the assistance of the priests and, especially, of the oracle.

For all of her life, she had a grudging respect and fear of the gods, but in her madness and embittered state of mind, she lost her fear and

Purity

believed herself to be invincible. She would now visit the temple and, if the answers she sought were not to her liking, then let the temple and all it contained go to the underworld.

Hang on a minute! If this nasty queen was so insular and she destroyed the wealth of the city and she broke off all alliances with all the other cities, how did they survive? Where did they get food from, for instance?

Oh, I don't know, my little angel. Maybe she kept in touch with some other nasty rulers in some other cities. Is this a fantasy or not? It is too late to start indulging in reality now, don't you think?

I suppose so. Where is she going next?

To the temple.

❈

The queen enters the inner sanctum of the temple. The oracle rises and bows. She does not. She stands aloof and regal. She has no guard with her, because even now, with her total disregard for others, she has a subconscious and begrudging respect for the temple and what it contains. She speaks:

"I greet you, Oracle."

"I greet you, your majesty."

The furniture in the chamber is meagre

And with bad grace and disdain she perches on a wooden stool. The oracle takes a seat.

"Now, Oracle. I do not want to waste time on idle chit-chat. I will come to my point. You are supposed to be the mirror of your people? Am I not correct?"

"That has been decreed since time immemorial, your majesty."

"Then, tell me, Oracle. What is the state of affairs? How do the people view me? Do they respect me?""

"They respect your power, your majesty."

"Are they in awe of me?"

"Indeed, your majesty. They are in awe of you."

"Do they fear me?"

"Their fear of you has no bounds, your majesty."

"But, Oracle, do they love me as they should."

"Why should they love you, your majesty?"

"Because of who and what I am. Because I am powerful and beautiful. Because it is in the nature of man to fear, respect and love those who are more powerful than themselves."

"Maybe that is the case with fear and respect, but I am afraid love has to be earned."

"What do they expect of me?"

"Justice and compassion. That is all."

"That is synonymous with weakness, Oracle. You wish me to become weak and grovelling like my dead husband? The masses can keep their love! Their fear will suffice! I hear they are worshipping the image of the princess within their houses in spite of the fact that I have forbid them to do so. Is this true?"

"So I have heard, your majesty."

"How do they feel about the princess?"

"The princess will always be in their hearts, your majesty. She has the love of her people. To them she is not only beautiful of face, but also pure and beautiful of spirit."

"You are taunting me, Oracle. Within this city I will not accept competition from others. You have to be careful. I may test my powers against the gods and then the temple will not be beyond my reach. You are the mirror of your people and I may just decide to break you."

"I am the truth, your majesty."

"It seems to me that the only way of subduing these common people is to search out their princess and destroy her."

She rises and leaves without another word.

The oracle waits until she has left, then he leaves his chamber in search of the high priest.

She is rather disturbed, this queen of ours, isn't she?

Oh, yes, my little flower. She is more than disturbed. She is quite evil. But, then it is a fact of life that both good and evil have a habit of turning in on themselves.

What do you mean?

Well, for example: if a person is good and treated all around with respect, then respect and kindness is often returned, even by those who are not naturally good and respectful. The same happens with evil. If you should surround yourself with evil, it is inevitable that you will eventually succumb to it. So, my angel, our little queen will have to tread carefully. As the oracle might put it: if you should scatter foul meat around you, the carrion birds will eventually come to roost with you.

That's rather good! I will remember that one. Now where are we going next?

Let's see what Purity, the hunter and the companions had been up to for the last year.

※

Purity arrived in the Land of the Canyon-Dwellers and she dwelt with these people for a year. For the first couple of weeks she rested and gathered her mental strength. She found this unexpectedly necessary, since she did not realise what toll the year in the wilderness had taken upon her. Her recuperation was aided, not only by the hunter and the companions, but also by the king who ruled here, as well as his subjects. The companions, (who were all of royal blood), had the ear of the king and on their arrival they had told him the story of Purity. A glorious welcome was extended to her and both the king and his people soon succumbed to her natural charm and fell under her spell.

The canyon was some twenty leagues in length and was situated on top of a high ridge that sloped down to the north and south. The inner walls of the canyon sloped steeply down to two plains that edged the wide riverbanks. The river flowed straight down the middle of the canyon. At each end the canyon narrowed. The two plains disappeared, leaving only enough room for the river to enter and exit the canyon. At these points a number of fortresses were situated. These served to repel possible invaders from entering the canyon by means of the river. There were also defences all along the two edges of the canyon. These guarded against attacks from the north and the south.

The people of the canyon lived on the riverbanks and on the two plains where they grazed their sheep and where they planted and harvested their fruits and grains. But, their real wealth came from the canyon walls and the river. Here could be found rich gold deposits. The gold from the riverbed was panned and collected and deep mine shafts extended into the walls of the canyon. From these the rich gold ore was mined and smelted and worked into the finest gold artefacts that Purity had ever seen. As with her own city, folk came from far and wide to trade.

The canyon was ruled over by a young king who was aided by his brother, the prince. He was a fair and just king and he reminded the princess very much of her beloved father. There was an instant rapport between herself and the king and they would spend many hours in conversation and debate. She especially enjoyed these, since she had been so deprived of intellectual conversation for so long.

But, it was the prince, the king's brother, who captured her heart. He was tall, lean and strong with handsome features and a fair complexion. At every opportunity they would seek out each other's company and they could frequently be seen strolling together along the banks of the river. It was soon obvious to all that a romance was blossoming between the young prince and the foreign princess.

The prince and the king were identical twins and, by rights they should have ruled as joint monarchs, but the young prince had no stomach for this. He was restless of nature and he spent long periods away from his homeland, seeking out knowledge and adventure. He was quite happy to leave his brother to his own devices and he would only involve himself in state affairs when his advice was sought.

One day, after Purity had been with the Canyon-Dwellers for some months, the subject of her return to and her reclamation of her city was broached. On this occasion, the king, the prince, the hunter and the companions were all present and the subject was widely discussed. Ultimately it was decided that envoys should be sent to other cities with the aim of asking for help in this matter. The hunter also reminded them that the queen had many spies and that she would inevitably become aware of their activities. If they should indulge in these matters, Purity's life would necessarily become endangered. It was therefore also decided that she should not travel outside the canyon without the protection of a strong guard.

And, so the quest for allies began. During the following months the prince, the hunter and the companions travelled with the princess to many cities where they struck bargains and alliances. All the folk they visited were fully aware of the riches in silver that was contained within her own city and many were prepared to offer help in return for generous payment.

And, thus a year passed and plans were well under way to prepare a great army to retake her city.

What about the queen's spies? Surely she would be aware of these activities by now. She would not relinquish her hold as easily as that!

You are absolutely right, my little darling. As I have mentioned before: she may be a vain woman, but she is far from stupid. Let us pay her a visit and see what she is up to.

※

The queen's spies had indeed brought news of Purity's activities and the queen decided that decisive action was called for. The princess had finally to be eliminated, but she soon realised that this would not be easy. Her spies informed her that the princess was always well protected when she left the canyon and that an assassination attempt would most certainly fail. She therefore decided that the time had come for her to take matters into her own hands. To this aim, she summoned the Weasel.

The weasel was a sly man and he was also a great coward. His cowardice necessitated the development of a most devious side of his nature in order to afford him protection. As is so often with evil people, the weasel and the queen disliked and distrusted each other, but they recognised in each other similar characteristics and they soon realised that each of them were dependent on the other for the furtherance of their own ambition.

After lengthy discussion, they decided on a plan. If Purity could not be eliminated outside the canyon, she should be confronted within her lair. They concluded that an attack on her would not be expected inside the canyon and that her protection here would be reduced. All that was needed was for someone to enter the canyon and wait for a chance to perform the deed. The weasel anxiously wished to know whom she would send. He was most fearful that she had him in mind to perform the task. But, he was most surprised and delighted when she told him that she would undertake the mission herself. She would leave the city, travel south and enter the canyon in disguise. He was to remain in the city and circulate a rumour that she was indisposed and that she would be laid up in the palace for some time and that she would see no visitors during this period. This he agreed to with alacrity.

Early the following morning, while it was still dark, she left the city in the company of two of her men. She was disguised as an elderly lady, the wife of one of the men. The guards at the gate thought them to be rough traders from the south and did not pay them much heed.

That is, most of the guards did not notice anything untoward, except for one. He was in the employ of the oracle. As with the queen, he also had his own spies. This guard was a young man who made a big pretence of being a staunch supporter of the queen. In reality he was a member of a very secret society that had come into existence during the last year. The aim of this society was the restoration of the crown.

Two things caught his sharp eye as the three travellers passed through the gates: the first concerned the loads that were carried. He saw that the woman was carrying nothing and that the men were borne down under their heavy loads. Now, he knew the folk from the south and he knew that this behaviour was alien to them. In his opinion the men were a lazy bunch, and under no circumstances would they allow themselves to act as donkeys whilst their women folk walked free and easy. The second matter concerned the way in which the woman bore herself. She did not walk like an old woman. Although her hair was grey and her shoulders stooped, she could not disguise her graceful and sprightly gait. He did not know who these people were, but he was sure of one thing: they were not who they pretended to be.

This man, then, being an individual of great initiative, presented himself to the captain of the guard. He said that he had seen some furtive movement on the plain and he requested permission to investigate. The captain assented to his request. The guard said that the activity seemed a long way off and that he might not be back until the morning.

He then saddled a horse and went in pursuit of the travellers. He took great care not to move so close to them that he would be noticed. But, as dusk fell, he saw a glimmer of firelight in the distance and he gathered that they had settled for the night and swiftly he moved in closer the better to observe them.

As he crouched outside the ring of light which was cast by the fire, he was greatly surprised at what he observed: at the fireside sat the two men and the dark queen. She had shed her old-woman's wig and he recognised her on the instant. He spent just enough time listening to their conversation to discover their destination and their purpose. Then, thoughtfully, he made his way back to the city. The news he carried had to be delivered to the oracle at the earliest opportunity.

What can the oracle do about it? He is stuck in the temple.

Is he, my darling? Let us see.

※

The oracle and the high priest are sitting in the inner courtyard of the temple.

"Will you take some wine, High Priest?"

"I will, thank you, Oracle."

The oracle fills two goblets and hands one to the priest.

"Tell me, Holy Father. What do you see around you?"

"A strange question, Oracle. But, let me see. I see the inner courtyard of the temple. In the middle of the courtyard there is a tree which overhangs a pond with fish in it. Through the branches of the tree I can see the rays of the sun. There are long shadows on the cobblestones. Will that do?"

"Now, tell me, Holy Father. What do you hear?"

The high priest listens: "Nothing, Oracle. I can hear nothing."

"Do you not find that strange, High Priest? The noises of the city penetrate to this inner sanctum and I frequently sit here and listen to the hustle and bustle of my people. It helps me to gauge the mood of the city. But, do you hear the silence, Holy Father? And, did you notice what was missing from the tree? Birds. There are no birds. Even the creatures of the sky have deserted the city."

"You are right, Oracle. Then, what do you conclude?"

"Our city is dying. It is fading fast."

"I am afraid you may be right, Oracle. But, what can we do about it?"

"Have you heard the latest news Holy Father?"

"I have heard some, Oracle, but will you tell me what you know?"

"As with the queen, I also have my spies. I have heard from them that the princess, Purity, is mustering an army in the south with the purpose of retaking the city."

"But, this is good news! Is it not?"

"Yes indeed, it is. But, remember the queen is also aware of this and it is said that she has strengthened the defences. And, very disturbing news has come to my ears."

"What news, Oracle?"

"From a spy in the palace and from another at the gates I have learnt that the queen has decided to take matters into her own hands. She has decided that the princess should be eliminated and she has taken this burden on herself. Some seven days ago she has left the city in disguise. If she should succeed, our city will be finally doomed. Those that have pledged their allegiance to the princess will surely not move against the queen if Purity was to die."

"I see what you mean, Oracle. Then, do you have a solution?"

"As I said before, High Priest: the gods do not seem to be forthcoming with much practical help, so it is up to us to take action on our own behalf and since it is now seven days since the queen has departed, the time for action can no longer be postponed".

"I agree, Oracle. But, why have you left it so late?"

"I needed some time to reflect, Father. As the old saying goes: The man who makes a judgement in haste is akin to a man who drinks a new wine too soon. They are both likely to end up with a severe headache.

"That is true. Now, tell me. No doubt you have come to a decision. So, what do you have in mind?"

"Tomorrow you must fly the black flag from the roof, the sign that someone is dying. You must circulate the rumour that it is I. I intend to leave the city and follow the queen. I need to get to the princess so that I may attempt to protect her. Keep me on my deathbed until I return."

"But, is this wise, Oracle? The gods have decreed that you should not leave the temple whilst you hold your present post!"

"I have done it once before, Holy Father, and they have not struck me down yet. Anyway, they appeared to have turned their eyes away from our city, so I seriously doubt that they would concern themselves with my actions."

"When will you leave?"

"I will leave tonight. I need to go into the city to make some arrangements."

The priest rises. "I hope you are right in what you are doing. But, you are correct. The gods are not helping, so I suppose it is up to us now. My blessing goes with you, Oracle."

He leaves the courtyard.

I imagine the queen's people will leave the temple in peace for the time being, won't they?

Most certainly, my little flower. Like most evil people, the queen's followers are also cowards. I don't believe they will move against the temple while the queen is away. Anyway, let's find out what the oracle has in mind.

※

An hour or so before curfew they are all assembled in a small room in a house in one of the back streets of the city. There are about twenty of them, all young and mostly men folk, but with a small group of women, (about five or six), amongst their number. Throughout the afternoon they had all made their way surreptitiously to this meeting place. Each had come singly and all of them had taken great care not to make themselves conspicuous to the neighbours. Now they are all here and they are waiting for one more. They are all perched on stools around a large table and at the head sits the man who is obviously their leader: the young guard. One of the men speaks:

"Who is it that we are waiting for?"

"It is a great man. A man who will lead us to freedom."

"Yes, but what do we call him?"

"We shall call him eminence. It is best for all that none should know his name." There comes a soft knock on the door. "I think he has arrived."

One of the men rises and, lifting the latch, opens the door. A middle-aged man, clean-shaven, with shoulder length hair enters the room. The young guard rises and all the others follow his example. The man moves to stand next to the guard at the top of the table. The guard offers him a seat, but he declines it with a wave of the hand.

"I will stand. I think better on my feet. Greetings to all of you. We have much to discuss and plan, so shall we start right away? Good. Now, before we start, are there any questions?"

One of the young men rises to his feet: "Yes. Who are you and how should we know to trust you?"

"Unfortunately I cannot divulge my name, but I have on my person something that will prove my trustworthiness." He removes a parchment from the folds of his cloak. "I come just recently from the temple and this has been given to me so that I should show it to you. It is the parchment on which has been inscribed the events of the birth of the princess, Purity. Normally it is kept in the inner chamber of the temple and is only privy to those in highest authority. It has the signature of the oracle and the high priest. On this occasion it has been entrusted to me so that I should prove my good faith."

The parchment is passed around the table and all nod their acceptance.

"Good. Now, shall we continue? We have much to discuss and we do not have much time. I know who you all are and I am also aware of the valuable work you have done. For the last year you have caused small disruptions in the city. Disruptions which made it difficult for the queen and her followers to function efficiently. But, soon the time will come for more decisive action. As you are all no doubt aware, the princess has been busy mustering an army in the south. It is rumoured that she has nearly accomplished this task. But, what you may not know is that the queen has left the city."

"But, surely, this is then a good time for us to rise against her!"

"No. We must not be hasty. She has left the weasel in charge of affairs and, if possible, he is even more ruthless than she. Our people are not yet well organised and if there were any sign of insurrection the weasel will crush them like flies and we may not be given a fresh opportunity, for they will be on their guard. Let us wait for the princess and her army. Then, whilst they attack from outside, we can offer effective opposition from within."

"Then, why has the queen left the city?"

"The plans of the princess have also come to her notice and she intends to stop her."

One of the women interrupts him: "But, how can we be sure of all this? What evidence is there that the queen has left the city? It is said that she is indisposed and is keeping to her bed."

The young guard rises and tells the tale of how he espied the queen and two men leaving the city. He also tells of how he followed them and what he overheard as they sat around the fire. Then the oracle continues:

It has also come to my ears that she wishes to dispose of Purity herself and our first and most urgent task is to prevent this. We must move fast, for she has a head start on us. What I need from you are three volunteers: One man and two women to travel with me and assist me."

"The young guard rose to his feet: "I wish to accompany you!"

"No, you cannot. You will be missed from your post and if your absence in the city is discovered, it will cause unnecessary suspicion."

"However, I know the southern lands better than most and we will be able to travel faster with this knowledge. Be not concerned. I will fake my death and thus absent myself from my duties. In these days there are many dead bodies to be found in this city. I will arrange for one of these to be found and mutilated so that it will not be recognised. My guard's identification will be placed around its neck. These people may be ruthless, but fortunately they are also very ignorant and there will be no difficulty in persuading them that I had been killed in a street brawl. I have another reason why I should go. My father was a merchant of this city and when I was a boy I travelled with him on many occasions to the south where he traded. He was one of those who was dispossessed and killed by the dark queen. So, you see, it will be some small measure of revenge to thwart and help to destroy her."

"So be it, then. Now, are there two women who wish to accompany us?"

All the women rose to their feet.

"I thank you for your valour, but unfortunately only two of you can accompany us."

The guard points to two of them: "I suggest that you two accompany us. You are the most experienced in weaponry and we may have need of your skills."

"So be it. Now, as for the rest of you: to you fall the task of mustering an army within the city. Gather together all those who are loyal to the princess and prepare them for battle. When the time comes it will be invaluable to have an army inside the city, ready to launch an attack from within. We will be certain to send regular news of our progress. And now, you must be on your way. The hour of curfew is nearly upon us. The four of us will remain here for the night and leave the city in the morning. May the gods go with you."

With short intervals they leave the room until only the four travellers remain.

The following morning two men and two women leave the city together. The guards who interview them do not understand them for they speak in a language of the south. They are mounted on sturdy ponies and the guards, who take them for a family from the south, let them through the gates.

What is going to happen to Purity?

I don't know, my darling. I'll see what comes into my head. I believe things may shortly come to a crunch.

But, I'll tell you something, my darling: before we rejoin Purity, let us follow the oracle and the queen on the trail.

After the queen and her two companions had left the city, they travelled on foot, but the queen soon wearied of their slow progress. On the second day a man on a mule cart approached them and the queen, feigning injury, lured him from his cart and he was slain by her two companions. Now, with the mule and cart as transport, they made much quicker progress and after five days they were approaching the great forest. They knew that they would soon be forced to abandon the cart since the tracks through the forest were too narrow, but once again fortune smiled upon them.

One evening, as one of the men was collecting kindling for the fire, he saw a faint glimmering of light in the distance and, on closer investigation, he found three men sitting around a fire with six horses tethered nearby. Swiftly he made his way back to his companions and informed them of what he had found. The queen decided that they should purloin the horses and, later that night when all was in darkness, they stalked up to the three travellers and killed them whilst they were asleep.

Since they now possessed horses, they abandoned the mule and cart and on the following day they entered the forest. They now moved swiftly and after a few days they reached the plane and, eventually, the mountains and the deep ravine. Here, with difficulty, they led the horses along the ledge and under the waterfall and across the ravine, but two of the horses were so frightened by the rushing water that they plunged to their death on the rocky riverbed below.

After crossing the ravine, they made their way down the mountain track until they reached the grassy plain and the plateau and ultimately, the village where Purity had lived and posed as a goddess. Here they decided to take their ease for a few days and also allow the horses to rest.

The queen ingratiated herself with the villagers and these simple folk who were anxious to impart their news to any who would listen, soon told her of the goddess-princess who lived amongst them. This was probably the most momentous thing that had ever taken place in the village and, as is the case in such circumstances, the story of the goddess-princess was embellished and amplified beyond belief. They told of how the harvest had flourished as never before. One man told of how his wife had been barren for five years, but that the goddess-princess had laid her hands on his wife's stomach and blessed her and that she had miraculously conceived and given birth to a twin boy and girl. An old man told of how he was sent to guard the sacred cave during the winter months and that the goddess-princess had visited him every night and protected him from evils: "Old and weak as I am, I never suffered from any coughs or sneezes or ailments that you could mention. She was indeed a true goddess."

The council had even decided to erect a stone statue in honour of her in the centre of the village.

To all this the queen listened with a suppressed, but rising anger. Her jealousy was newly and harshly inflamed. So, after four days she made haste to be away from this place. With a new determination she set forth on the trail of her vengeance.

The rest of her journey was uneventful and thirty days after leaving the city, she and her two companions reached the land of the Canyon-Dwellers. Since many came from far and wide to visit this place and since this particular party's disguises were very good, they had no difficulty in gaining entrance to the canyon where they faded into the crowds and hid themselves amongst the many traders.

And, here we will leave them for a while, my beloved.

The oracle must be shortly on her heels?

Yes, indeed, my darling. Let us see how he is faring.

In their pursuit of the dark queen, the oracle and his travelling companions were better prepared than those who went before them. The young guard had arranged for horses to be left tethered in a small copse not far from the city. They soon took possession of these and they swiftly traversed the distance between the city and the dark forest. The guard did indeed know his way about the lands and they passed through the forest without difficulty and then across the grasslands to the distant hills and the ravine. On reaching the ravine they had the foresight to blinker the horses so that they may be unaware of the dangers of the crossing and without too much fuss they crossed to the other side and down the hills onto the plains below.

As with Purity and the dark queen who went before them, they also stopped to rest at the village of the harvesting folk and once again they had to listen to their tale. No need to say that with each day the tales were more gloriously distorted. It was inevitable that the legend of the goddess-princess would eventually pass into their folklore and remain their forever as a mythical indication of their glorious history.

The oracle who, in spite of his disguise, could not rid himself of the demeanour of authority, dined on an evening with the chief of the elders and the following conversation ensued:

"Tell me, Master: are you aware of the true character of the goddess who visited you?"

"Oh, indeed I am! I know that she is a princess from a far land who was forced into flight. I also know that there was no harm in her and that the evil resides in those who brought about her misfortune."

"And, what about the people? Is it right that they should afford a mere human such elevated standing? Are you not afraid that the true gods may frown on such impudence?"

"No. I do not believe so, my friend. A community of people is like a pond of water. If the pond is deprived of regular fresh water it will eventually stagnate and become barren and dry. It is the same with us. We need events such as these in order to replenish our collective spirit. Could it not be argued that the coming of this girl to our village was due to the direct intervention of the gods?"

"You may very well be right, Master. And, I can only wish for a prosperous future for you and your folk. But, to change tack for a while: did you have the company of a small group in the last few days?"

"Could you describe this company in greater detail? Our village lies close to the main road that passes across the plane and many a traveller takes his ease for a while with us."

"It would be difficult to describe them since I am sure that they would be disguised. However, I believe that there would have been three people in the company – two men and one woman. The woman is of a startling beauty and very dark of complexion."

"Yes, indeed! Such a company had been here, no more than a few days ago. But, tell me: what is your concern with them?"

"I trust that you know the whole tale concerning the princess?"

"Only some of it. Will you tell it all?"

And, so the oracle related all, since the birth of the princess until the present.

"I believe that the company who stayed with you are none other than the dark queen and some of her followers. I also believe that they are in pursuit of the princess and that they mean her harm. In turn, my companions and I are in pursuit of the queen and we shall attempt to forestall her."

"I wish you success. But, how can we be of assistance to you?"

"You cannot help me, but it has come to my hearing that the princess is raising an army in the south and that she will shortly attempt an invasion of her city. If you truly honour the princess I would ask that you should aid in any small way those who would dedicate themselves to this task."

"In this matter you have the full commitment of my people. We will do all we can to protect and honour the princess, for is she not our princess-goddess?"

After only a few days rest the oracle and his companions went on their way and as was with the queen, they completed the rest of their journey uneventfully. They arrived at the land of the Canyon-Dwellers only one day after the queen.

Will he save her?

God knows.

But, without Purity there is no story!

Remember, my darling! This is a myth and most myths end tragically! I personally believe that a good tragedy is more thought provoking than a story that ends with everybody living happily ever after. Anyway, be that as it may, this is your story and I will do my best for the princess.

A short distance from the main town that straddles the river (on the north bank of the river), stands a large spread of houses and lanes. In appearance this quarter differs a great deal from the town where the local people reside.

The streets and avenues of the canyon town are wide and straight and tree-lined. The houses are well kept with small but elegant gardens where shrubs and plants of all kinds could be viewed in a glorious display of colours. The market square is spacious and clean and surrounded by flowerbeds and fountains and statues of all kinds.

In contrast, this other town consists of a conglomerate of housing, inns and shops where disorder appears to be the order of the day. The spaces between the dwellings are pierced by a confusion of narrow streets and alleyways that seem to lead to nowhere in particular. It is here that all the travelling salesmen and buyers reside. Daily they would travel the short distance to the market where they would peddle their wares, but whatever they could not sell, they would dispose of at knocked-down prices in the little shops of the conurbation.

The king was most dissatisfied with this arrangement. He considered this mishmash of dwellings to be an eyesore and not at all in keeping with the rest of the canyon. He vowed that he would have all of it pulled down and tastefully rebuilt as soon as this venture with the princess was at an end.

It is here, in a tavern, that a small group is gathered around a table. Many folk from all different lands are gathered in the tavern and a great variety of dialects can be heard. At regular intervals someone would rise to his feet and perform a medley on a drum or a flute or a harp. Others would sing songs or recite poetry. Each performance is greeted with loud cheers and applause. Serving wenches are rushing among the crowds, plying all with wine and food.

In all this noise the group gathered around a table in one corner of the tavern has no fear of being overheard. One of them speaks:

"May I ask for a name? And, why am I brought here in such secrecy?"

"I regret that I cannot reveal my name to you. Suffice it to say that my friends and I are here in the name of our beloved city in the north and, as it is with you, we have the welfare and prosperity of the princess, Purity, at the centre of our hearts."

"How should I know the truth of any of this?"

"Ah, Hunter! I understand and admire your caution. You have never been one to put your trust in others and since your recent confrontation with the dark queen, it is inevitable and quite understandable that you should be lacking in faith in those around you. But, I have a parchment here that should assure you of my good intentions."

A scroll is handed over and perused.

"But, surely! This is the birth scroll of the princess Purity! How did you obtain this?"

"It has been handed to me by those in authority in the temple, to be used in circumstances such as this to prove my good faith."

"Then I have no choice but to put my trust in you. Will you then answer my second query: what is it that you require of me?"

"Ah, well. That is an easier question to answer and I will come straight to the point. There is no need to scrabble amongst the hedges with this. The dark queen has left the city."

"Do you mean by that that she has resigned the city? But, surely! If this is so then it is excellent news!

"I am afraid not, my friend. She has left her henchmen in charge. She has left the city in order to pursue the princess. At this very moment she is here in the canyon and we can take it for granted that she is not here to bear gifts. She is here to dispose of the princess."

"Mm. There are matters to consider here. Since we know that she is here in the canyon, could we not find her and take her into our charge? I believe this to be a gods sent opportunity to rid ourselves of her!"

"You are right in one respect, Hunter. Find her we must, but unfortunately we cannot detain her. Remember, her thugs are still in command of the city and although they may leave if their queen does not return, I believe that they may do much slaughtering of our people before they go. No. I believe that it would be better to overthrow them together with their queen. But, we must find her and prevent her from doing harm to the princess."

"How long has it been since she arrived here?"

"Two days. So we must be swift. I do not believe that she will take long to act. Fortunately, she is a vain and beautiful woman and with intensive searching she should not be difficult to find. It is my guess that her vanity will not make her take kindly to disguises."

"Yes. I agree. Well, there is no time to lose. I will be on my way to set things in motion."

"Before you go, there are some other small matters that I seek your help with."

They talk together for some time and then the hunter gets up and leaves the tavern. The four remaining conspirators make pretence of joining in the revelry for some time and then they also retire.

How are they going to find her? I presume that she is living in this awful town with all the other travellers and from your description it sounds as if they will be looking for the proverbial needle in the haystack.

That is not my problem, my darling. Remember, he has the companions to help him. They better find her, otherwise, my angel, our Purity is up the proverbial creek without a paddle.

Well! What are you waiting for! This is beginning to get exciting.

※

The canyon was not like any other city. There were no man-made walls. Instead the people had the cliffs and the fortresses for protection. The people were safely scattered over a large area of riverbanks and plains. However, a daily market was arranged in the canyon town on one of the riverbanks. Here the people came to trade their wares of fruit and animals. Here also those strangers who were allowed into the canyon came to buy the many gold artefacts which were produced by the inhabitants.

The relationship between the people and the king and prince was of a remarkably intimate nature. The king and the prince did not believe in hiding themselves away in their palace. They could frequently be found in places of entertainment, as well as other public places, fraternising with their subjects. Often they would wander amongst the market stalls, joking and bartering with the stallholders and during the last year, the young princess usually accompanied them.

Purity had recently returned from a city where she had procured the services of an army. All was now in place and it was only required to finalise the plans.

It was seven days after the meeting in the tavern and Purity was having her morning meal and her spirits were high. The young prince entered her room and invited her to join him in a walk through the market. She readily accepted and all morning they walked and waved and talked to the people.

Eventually they came to a stall where an old woman was selling the most succulent looking fruit. Purity and the prince decided on buying

Purity

some peaches. The old woman refused to take any money from them. Instead, she searched through her fruit and selected the largest and most beautiful peaches which she packed into a small basket and these she presented to them. The prince and the princess accepted the gift with gratitude.

As they continued on their way, Purity removed one of the peaches from the basket and determined to eat it. As she raised the peach to her mouth, a woman knocked against her and the peach fell from her hand and the rest of the fruit were spilled from the basket. With many apologies the woman insisted on picking up the fallen fruit, but what none noticed was that she replaced the fruit with others that she kept concealed in her apron. Thanking the woman kindly, Purity took the newly filled basket from her and she and the prince went on their way.

Finding a place on the riverbank, they decided to rest for a while. Once again Purity removed one of the peaches and ate it with relish. No sooner had she finished the last morsel when her face grew pale and she clutched at her stomach. The prince, in the utmost alarm, immediately carried her back to the palace where she was confined to her bed.

A new doctor from a distant land, but with many qualifications, had recently joined the palace staff and he was immediately summoned. He insisted that he should be left alone with the princess and that he would do his best for her. But, after only a few minutes he returned to the anxiously waiting crowd and informed them sombrely that the princess had passed from this world.

At the same time as the princess was carried into the palace, before the news of Purity's death could reach the ears of the population, two men and a woman hastily left the city.

Oh, dear! What are you doing? You cannot kill the main character off like that!

Why not, my little flower? Our story is nearly at an end. The people will most likely get their city back and as it is said, surely the needs of the many outweigh the needs of the few.

Well, I am not going to allow you to leave things in this most unsatisfactory manner! This will not do!

Well, leave it to me, my angel and I will see what can be done.

✤

A chamber in the palace. Present are the king, the prince and some generals. The king speaks:

"I welcome you all to this conference. I wish that our meeting could have taken place under happier circumstances. The death of the princess is indeed regrettable and most deplorable. Although I myself and my subjects have only known her for a brief year, I can assure you that she will be sorely missed by all. In my opinion this heinous crime had been committed, not only against a royal personage, but also against the rightful ruler of a state and I therefore believe that it should be avenged. For, is it not so that, if this crime should go unpunished, those who perpetrated it will believe themselves able to act with equally bad grace towards other heads of state?"

One of the generals speaks: "The events of the last few days are most regrettable and we all offer our sincere condolences on the death of the princess. However, this event casts everything in a different light. If we should be successful in relieving the city, what guarantees are there to ensure payment for our efforts?"

"You do not need to have any concerns about this matter. I have it from the highest authority of those who resist the queen that you will be paid in full. And, if by chance they should not honour their word, I give you my pledge that I will personally settle this debt. Documents to this effect will be drawn up and signed by me."

"We have always known you to be an honourable man and we accept your word on this matter.

All nod in agreement.

"I thank you. Now, shall we proceed with the plans for battle? First we need to know exactly how many men we will have at our disposal.

Another general speaks: "Between us we will be able to supply in the region of fifteen thousand men, five thousand on horse and ten thousand foot-soldiers."

"That is good. I can muster about five thousand men, four thousand foot-soldiers and one thousand on horse. That makes a total force of twenty thousand."

"Can we rely on any support from within the city?"

The young guard from the city speaks: "Yes, but their strength is not entirely certain. Rumours have it that it could be from one thousand to five thousand. I believe we would be better served to err on the lesser side. So, we will have a combined force of approximately twenty-one thousand."

"What is the strength of the queen's forces?"

"Once again we are not certain, but it is thought that she may have some thirty thousand under her command."

"That is not good. They outnumber us by three to two."

"I agree. We would have to rely to a certain extent on surprise and to do so we will have to move swiftly. The dark queen has only recently left for home and if we could follow shortly on her heels and attack the city, she will not have time to adequately organise her troops."

"That is true, but unfortunately, it will take at least seven days for us to return to our own cities and assemble our own armies."

"I am aware of that fact. However, my men are ready and we can leave on the morrow. Being a relatively small force, we can also move fast. I suggest that we go ahead and besiege the city to the best of our ability and for as long as we can. With some luck, we should be able to contain them until you arrive with reinforcements.

A third general speaks: "It may take us some time to come to your assistance. Have you decided on a plan to hold the city until such time? It is most important that you should contain the queen within the city until we arrive. Under no circumstances should we want to encounter such a great force on the open plains, for we shall surely be overwhelmed."

"No. Not yet. But, we are fortunate in that we have those with us who know the terrain and with their help I am certain that the method will come to us."

"Well, there is no more to be said, then. We will leave as soon as possible in order to set our own plans in motion."

"That is good. But, I suggest that you stay with us tonight and leave with us in the morning. We can provide the protection of our army at least for some of the way. You are all invited to dine with me tonight. May the gods of justice look favourably on us."

The generals rise and leave the room. Only the king and his brother remain. The king speaks:

"What do you think? Can they be relied upon?"

"I think so. Obviously, it will depend to a large extent on how successfully we can hold the city until they arrive. If they should find us in disarray and beaten, they may very well lose heart. On the other hand, if we could contain the queen's troops successfully, I am certain that they will join us whole-heartedly in the battle."

"Then it is up to us to make sure that we succeed. As I said to the generals, we are fortunate that we have with us the hunter and the companions. They know the terrain and I am certain that they will be able to devise a stratagem to aid our success."

"Shall I call them? Do you wish to discuss these matters with them tonight?"

"No. That will not be necessary. It will take us some three weeks to reach the city. We will have enough time on the road to perfect our plan of action. And now, let us retire and prepare for dinner. The gods only know when we will be able to eat in civilised conditions again."

They leave the room.

The odds are rather stacked against them. How on earth are they going to hold the city with only five thousand men?

Well, my little flower. Let us swiftly move on and see what they are going to do.

As the sun rose the next morning, an ensemble left the canyon. It consisted of an army of five thousand, or so, accompanied and led by the king of the canyon-dwellers. In this grand procession could also be found the prince, the hunter and the companions. The two largest portions of the army were under the direction of the king and the prince, both men being well versed in battle. The rest of the army was placed in equal proportion under the command of the hunter and the companions.

For three weeks they travelled north, following the route that Purity had so painstakingly followed some two years ago. It was inevitable that news of their progress should proceed them and some thousand fighting men joined them on their way. These mainly consisted of those who were of a mercenary disposition. They believed that there might be rich pickings to be had at the defeat of the silver city. Although welcoming these reinforcements, the king cautioned himself and his generals as to their reliability. He was well acquainted with human nature and he realised that most of these stragglers would desert at the first sign of trouble.

Their progress was swift and within one moon they reached the forest that led to the great plain. At this point they were forced to move at a slower pace. It was not only the men and the horses that slowed them. Travelling behind the army were the mules and carts that carried the provisions and the heavy loads they carried created a considerable impedance to their progress. They finally reached the outskirts of the forest where they halted. They were now about to enter onto the great plain that lay before the city. Here they encamped for three days whilst formalising their plans of besiegement. This, then, is what they did.

The king in his shrewdness realised that news of their march and the approximate strength of the army would be carried to the queen by her spies. He therefore took only the thousand men on horseback under his command and approached the city across the plains. These plains were vast and it took another three days to reach the city. They travelled in a most disorganised fashion, giving the impression that indiscipline was rife amongst the ranks. He believed that the spies would report a mass desertion by the rest of the army and that these were only the remnants determined on an assault on the city. The rest of the army fragmented into small groups and followed, only travelling by night. Now, for the rest of the scheme, the king depended on the complacency that the approach of his small army might induce in the mind of the queen and in this he was correct.

On reaching the city he struck a most disorderly camp. His men were scattered over a wide area, apparently oblivious to any danger or command from their officers. Indiscriminate fires were lit and constant brawls broke out amongst the soldiers. All this acted as distractions to the queen's men who watched and jeered from the city walls. This band of men appeared to be in such a disorganised state that the queen's soldiers treated them with the utmost disdain, to the extent that they could not bother themselves with sending a force against them. In all, this is exactly what the king had in mind.

About the northern entrance to the city he did not concern himself over much. He learnt from the hunter that approach to and from these gates by way of circumventing the city was practically impossible. This was indeed a mistake on the part of the king and he was soon to regret his lack of attention to the north gate.

All that day taunts and jeers were exchanged between the king's men and the queen's soldiers. At nightfall, (after much drink had apparently been consumed), the fires were extinguished and the camp fell silent. During the hours of darkness the rest of the army approached.

Some miles from the city gates there were two wooded areas to left and right. In these woods the soldiers under the command of the prince, the hunter and the companions secreted themselves. This was done with the utmost care and stealth and none in the city was aware of their presence.

The next morning at dawn some of the king's men made their approach close to the gates and fired some arrows and threw some spears at the soldiers on the walls. This was done more as a taunt rather than a serious assault. They kept up this manoeuvre all morning, retreating swiftly out of range of the missiles from the walls after each attack. By noon the soldiers on the wall appeared to have had their fill of these taunts and as the king watched, the gates were suddenly flung wide and a contingent of approximately three thousand on horseback pursued his men. This was exactly the eventuality he had hoped for. Rapidly his men were gathered in a close formation and they swiftly retreated from the enemy, leading them away from the city and along the corridor formed by the two woodland areas. With a sense of dismay the onlookers on the walls saw the disaster that then befell their companions. Without warning a great army of men suddenly appeared from the woods. In no time at all the queen's men found themselves totally surrounded. Their retreat to the city was cut off. A short but fierce battle followed in which all of the queen's soldiers were slaughtered. Some tried to make their escape onto the plains and some tried to return to the city, but all were pursued and mercilessly cut down.

After this short but bloody battle the king's men regrouped and returned to their camp.

Those who watched from the walls now saw before them a vast army of men and they were filled with apprehension. This was indeed what the king had in mind. The queen's commanders would now be reluctant to attempt any sorties on his army. He now felt certain that he could detain them within the city until such time as the allies arrived.

And so, the siege of the silver city began. None knew how long it would take for reinforcements to arrive, but all were sure that it would be some time. The once apparently undisciplined group of one thousand men were now a well-disciplined army of six thousand and this fact was eminently obvious to the watchers on the wall. At night great fires were lit and many guards were posted, making it impossible for surprise attacks.

On the fourth day of the siege the king watched with surprise as the gates were opened and ten men on horseback emerged, all carrying white flags. They advanced to the edge of the camp where they were halted by the guards. The leader of the ten then produced a parchment which he handed to one of the guards, saying that he had been instructed to deliver a letter from the queen of the silver city to the king of the canyon-dwellers. The letter was swiftly conveyed to the king and he retired to his tent to read it. This is what it said:

"From: Her Royal Highness, Revered Queen of the Silver City."

"To: His Royal Highness, King of the Canyon-Dwellers."

"My Liege,

"I find it most distressing having to send this missive to you. I can say in all honesty that I am at a loss to understand your present demeanour towards me and mine. I do not understand your motives for besieging my city. I have at no time that I am aware of intended any harm towards yourself. If, however, I have caused you inadvertent offence, I wish to convey my sincere apologies.

"Why do you not gather your men and return to your land? If you should do this I will give you my word that I will overlook this most unfortunate incident. I also have it in mind that we will both be better served in an alliance. Your land is rich in gold and my city is renowned for its silver deposits. Why should we indulge in fighting when, as allies, we could be of great benefit to each other? Indeed, both you and I have the opportunity to acquire wealth beyond measure.

"I hope that you will look favourably on my request and I await your reply with hopeful anticipation."

The king pondered on the queen's words for some time and then he constructed the following reply:

"From: His Royal Highness, King of the Canyon-Dwellers"

"To: The Treacherous Impostor"

"The reason for me besieging your city is because of what you are: A traitor and an impostor. I have an absolute aversion to rats, but you, my lady, make even these vermin as creatures appear pure and clean. It is my belief that, in order to make this a safer and better world for all, you should be exterminated with the same passion that I would employ to rid myself of a rat.

"The erstwhile king of this city was a friend to me and to all of those who live in these lands. Not only did you murder him and procured his throne by deceit, but also did you cause the death of his daughter, Purity, a young person who was pure of spirit and fair of face, unlike yourself who is the epitome of all evil.

"Now, I have a proposal of my own: why do you not leave this city at once and take your evil followers with you. I give you my promise that, if you should do so, I will not pursue you. On the other hand, if you should not accede to my request, you will suffer the full force of my retribution."

This letter was handed to the queen's men and they returned to the city. Needless to say, no more was heard from the queen and the siege continued.

The counter-attack on the king's men happened a week later. It was swift and it took them all totally by surprise. It happened just as dawn was breaking.

The soldiers were stirring from their sleep when a loud trumpet blast was heard from the south. All ran out of their tents and began to cheer. They believed it to be the reinforcements come to join them, but as they looked their cheering died away and they were overcome with dismay. A great phalanx of soldiers were rushing towards them and at the head was carried the banner of the dark queen. Also, behind them the city gates sprang open and a horde of men were pouring onto the plain. In their turn they were now surrounded.

But, this is preposterous! You are going to let the dark queen win! Where did all those soldiers come from? Did the allied generals betray the king?

I don't know yet if the queen is going to win, my darling. And, no. The generals did not betray the king. All those soldiers are the queen's men.

But, how did they get out of the city?

Well, it was really quite easy, my angel. You see, the king underestimated the dark queen. She might be evil, but she is definitely not stupid. This is how she did it.

Remember what I told you about the defences of the city. To the south are the plains across which an enemy can be seen for miles. Also, there are the defensive walls. To the east and the west there are high cliffs and it would be very difficult for any army to scale these without notice and without being repelled. But, what the king did not take into account was the fact that it was possible to leave the city unobserved.

The queen's soldiers left the city by the north gate. They travelled some miles to the east until they came across a fast flowing stream. They entered the riverbed and made their way downstream to the plain. You see, it was a fast flowing stream and no army of men would have made it along this riverbed up the mountain that surrounded the city. But, with some difficulty it was indeed possible to descend. In the process they lost a number of men and horses, but they made it to the plains and this is how they managed to attack the king's forces from the south.

Well, I don't know how you are going to do it, but you better get the king out of this mess.

Alright, my flower. Don't fret. I'll see what I can do.

This, then, in brief were the events of the battle: as earlier described, the king's army was raised from their slumbers by a trumpet call and they suddenly found themselves under attack from the south. And then, the city gates flew open and another group of soldiers were descending upon them from the city. They were trapped and in danger of being surrounded. However, the gods favoured them in two ways, firstly, their own discipline. The king had the foresight to place a large number of soldiers on guard duty and with bow and arrow and throwing spear they managed to keep the enemy at bay until such time as the rest of the army could gather themselves. Fortunately they were well trained and it was not long before they could join the battle.

The second way in which they were favoured was the relative indiscipline of the queen's men. Instead of spreading out and trying to outflank the king's men, they charged headlong into battle in close formation. Consequently they provided an easy target and the first onslaught was soon repelled. But, the queen's men were numerous and soon this advantage began to tell. Although many were slaughtered by the long range missiles, the queen's men eventually managed to penetrate this rain of death and they were now in hand to hand combat with their adversaries. The king realised that his men would soon be overwhelmed.

Then, a third event took place that at least gave him a respite. A great cry came from within the city and the king saw that the queen's soldiers on that side were retreating. The king instantly knew what had happened. The citizens of the city were coming to his assistance. He could now divert more of his troops towards the attack from the south, but he knew that he could not withstand them for too long. Their numbers were too great.

Then, another trumpet blast penetrated through the noise of the battle. The king believed this to be the call for the final assault on his battle-wearied men, but as he raised his eyes to the battle in front of him, a great cry of joy escaped him. In the distance he saw a cloud of dust which was rapidly moving towards them. The allies had arrived! His officers had also seen the approaching armies and with renewed vigour they urged on their men.

Of the rest of their battle there is not much to report. Within a short space of time the queen's men were surrounded. Most of them soon realised the futility of further fighting, but many scattered and fled across the plains. It has to be remembered that most of these men were mercenaries and bandits before they joined the queen and fleeing from the battle was no dishonour to them. They would suffer no pangs of guilt or hardship. It would not take them long to join other marauding bands of the plains and they would soon enough fall comfortably into their previous mode of existence.

Only one more event took place on this momentous day which is worth reporting: from the open gates came a group on horseback and in the middle of them rode the queen. She was dressed from head to foot in black and she was mounted on a stallion that was as black as the night. She was surrounded by her personal bodyguard and behind her rode her lance bearer. No one would ever know for certain what her intentions were. It was evident from her demeanour that she did not intend to sue for peace, for with a great cry she drew her sword and led a charge on the king's army.

Purity

Then came the final happening of the day; an event so momentous in its import that many remembered it with wonder and it was to be related for generations to come. The men in front of the charging queen moved to left and right and from within the parting ranks came a rider on a white horse. It was a woman and she was dressed in white. Next to this figure loped a great silver tiger. She raised her white veil and the dark queen recognised her on the instant. It was the princess, Purity. And, with this recognition, the queen's already distorted mind failed her completely. With a cry of horror, fear and hatred, all mingled together, she charged blindly at the white spectre, her sword held high in both hands. All around were frozen into immobility. As she reached the princess, she steadied herself for the stroke that would finally split the princess's head in two and would rid her from her enemy for all times. But, then, in a streak of silver the tiger leapt. It struck at the horses head and scored it across its eyes. With a shriek of terror and pain the defenceless animal reared onto its hind legs. The queen, grasping her sword with both hands, was unbalanced and she fell backwards, right onto the lance held by the lance bearer. It passed straight through her body and emerged between her breasts. For some moments she hung, suspended on the end of the lance. Then, the lance bearer, staring in horror, lowered the weapon and she slid free and fell to the ground where she laid motionless.

However, she did not die on the instant. She raised herself on one elbow and looked back at the city that for so longed personified all her dreams and ambitions and, as she looked at the two ornamental tigers that stood guard upon the city walls, she saw their eyes glowing with a most malevolent gleam. With a final cry of horror she fell back and breathed her last.

I thought Purity was dead. Where did she spring from?

I think we should pay the oracle a final visit, don't you, my little flower? I see his hand in this. He has some explaining to do.

"Well, Oracle. I believe you have some explaining to do. Rumours had reached us of the demise of the princess. How did you manage to bring her back to life?"

"She never died, High Priest, but I have to admit, it was a close thing. We followed the dark queen to the land of the Canyon-Dwellers and there the hunter and the companions kept a close eye on her. Whether she became aware of the fact that she was under observation I cannot say, but somehow she gave them the slip and I nearly missed her when she set up her stall in the market square, but one of the women who travelled with us spotted her. With her woman's eye she recognised the disguise on the instant. I knew that the princess liked to wander through the market and taste the fruits and I predicted, (correctly as it turned out), what the queen's intentions were. Fortunately, I had my medicines and drugs with me and I applied a sleeping drug to some fruit. When I saw the princess taking fruit from the queen, I arranged for it to be knocked from her hands and it was replaced with my own. She ate the fruit and went into a deep sleep. I had arranged a post for myself at the palace as a doctor (obviously with the full knowledge of the king and the prince). I had her taken to an inner room of the palace and there I declared her dead. Once again, the king and the prince were fully informed."

"But, why, Oracle? What was the point to all this? Surely, you took a great risk? There was a possibility that the allied generals might not join the battle, for instance."

"That was a chance I had to take. Above all I felt it my duty to ensure the safety of the princess. As long as she was known to be alive, the queen would not rest. She was a most resourceful woman and in the end she would have succeeded in murdering her. But, once she believed the princess, Purity, to be dead, she would return to the city. Then, it was up to the king to persuade the generals to continue with the alliance and this he did successfully. We spirited the princess away and she joined one of the following generals. The rest you know."

"Yes, I do. And, a most satisfactory conclusion to everything. It is only one week since the battle, but already the gloomy atmosphere in the city has lifted. There is still a lot to be done, though. I understand that there is a strong romance blossoming between our princess and the king's brother. I have only met the young man once, but I was impressed by his amiability and his shrewdness. It won't be long before he takes his place as king beside our new queen and I have no doubt that they will cure the ails of our city and our people."

"I am sure you are right, High Priest. But, now I must return to my duties as oracle of the people and my first duty is to write the obituary to the dark queen. I know that she was evil and that in her madness she nearly ruined our city, but tradition dictates that she should be honoured with a royal burial."

"Then, go to it, Oracle. But, before I leave you in peace, will you tell me one thing? Did you enjoy your time in the world? You know, now that I see you without your hair and beard, I am reminded of just what a handsome figure you strike."

"I thank you, High Priest. I must admit, I did notice the odd wench casting a favourable eye in my direction. Yes, I did enjoy myself for a brief spell. But, I am happy to return to the temple and its security. I feel a profound sympathy for my people. On the face of it the world provides so much excitement, but there are also so many pitfalls. No. I think I am better off here where I can help the people to combat these."

"Tell me. Do you think the city would have survived if the dark queen had remained on the throne?'

"Strangely, yes, High Priest. You see, I think of a city and its people as being like an animal. Keep a tiger in a cage and feed it regularly and it will obey you, but if you should torture it as well, you should never turn your back on it. It will eventually find a way of striking back."

And so, my angel, we have reached the end of our tale.

Thank you. I did enjoy it. I seemed to have heard a similar story before, though.

You probably have, my darling. But, you know, as the saying goes, there is nothing new under the sun. In music there are only so many notes to an octave. It is the order you play them in which dictates the melody. The same with stories. There are only so many words and events. Arrange them in a different way and you have a different story. And, now we must rest.

What will your next story be?

Sometime I will tell you the story of a young girl who lived a most terrible life.

What happened to her?

When she was young her mother died. She was brought up by her father who was very rich. But, when she was ten he died as well and she was taken into care by her aunt and uncle. She inherited all her father's wealth, but it was put in trust with her uncle and aunt as executors. They had two daughters who treated the young orphan girl appallingly. The uncle and aunt also treated her as a servant and they squandered all her money.

This one also sounds vaguely familiar.

As I said, my little angel, there is nothing new under the sun. Now, go to sleep, my precious.

Yes, I will go to sleep now. That was a lovely story. I think I will have good dreams tonight. Thank you, my lovely daddy.

The End.